Just as Long as We're Together

OTHER YEARLING BOOKS YOU WILL ENJOY:

YEARLING BOOKS/YOUNG YEARLINGS/YEARLING CLASSICS are designed especially to entertain and enlighten young people. Charles F. Reasoner, Professor Emeritus of Children's Literature and Reading, New York University, is consultant to this series.

For a complete listing of all Yearling titles, write to Dell Readers Service, P.O. Box 1045, South Holland, Illinois 60473.

Just as Long as We're Together

Together

❀

JUDY BLUME

A YEARLING BOOK

Published by
Dell Publishing
a division of
The Bantam Doubleday Dell Publishing Group, Inc.
666 Fifth Avenue
New York, New York 10103

The lyrics on page 162 are from SIDE BY SIDE MCMXXVII
Shapiro Bernstein & Co., Inc. New York.
Copyright renewed. Used by permission.

ISBN: 0-440-70013-2

Reprinted by arrangement with Judy Blume and Orchard
Books, a division of Franklin Watts, Inc.

Printed in the United States of America

One previous Dell edition 40075
Book Club edition
New Dell edition
September 1988

10 9 8 7 6 5 4 3 2 1
KRI

To my friend,

STEPHEN MURPHY

who touched my life
with his courage, dignity
and never-ending sense of humor

Lola will always remember . . .

Hunks

"Stephanie is into hunks," my mother said to my aunt on Sunday afternoon. They were in the kitchen making potato salad and I was stretched out on the grass in our yard, reading. But the kitchen window was wide open so I could hear every word my mother and aunt were saying. I wasn't paying much attention though, until I heard my name.

At first I wasn't sure what my mother meant by *Stephanie is into hunks*, but I got the message when she added, "She's taped a poster of Richard Gere on the ceiling above her bed. She says she likes to look up at him while she's trying to fall asleep at night."

"Oh-oh," Aunt Denise said. "You'd better have a talk with her."

"She already knows about the birds and the bees," Mom said.

"Yes, but what does she know about boys?" Aunt Denise asked.

It so happens I know plenty about boys. As for hunks, I've never known one personally. Most boys my age—and I'm starting seventh grade in two weeks—are babies. As for my Richard Gere poster, I didn't even know he was famous when I bought it. I got it on sale. The picture must have been taken a long time ago because he looks young, around seventeen. He was really cute back then. I love the expression on his face, kind of a half-smile, as if he's sharing a secret with me.

Actually, I don't call him Richard Gere. I call him Benjamin but my mother doesn't know that. To her he's some famous actor. To me, he's Benjamin Moore, he's seventeen and he's my first boyfriend. I love that name—Benjamin Moore. I got it off a paint can. We moved over the summer and for weeks our new house reeked of paint. While my room was being done I slept in my brother's room. His name is Bruce and he's ten. I didn't get a good night's sleep all that week because Bruce has nightmares.

Anyway, as soon as the painters were out of

my room I moved back in and taped up my posters. I have nineteen of them, not counting Benjamin Moore. And he's the only one on the ceiling. It took me all day to arrange my posters in just the right way and that night, as soon as my mother got home from work, I called her up to see them.

"Oh, Stephanie!" she said. "You should have used tacks, not tape. Tape pulls the paint off the walls."

"No, it doesn't," I said.

"Yes, it does."

"Look . . . I'll prove it to you," I said, taking down a poster of a lion with her cubs. But my mother was right. The tape did pull chips of paint off the wall. "I guess I better not move my posters around," I said.

"I guess not," Mom said. "We'll have to ask the painters to touch up that wall."

I felt kind of bad then and I guess Mom could tell because she said, "Your posters do look nice though. You've arranged them very artistically. Especially the one over your bed."

Rachel

"I can't believe this room!" my best friend, Rachel
Robinson, said. She came over the second she
got home from music camp. We shrieked when
we saw each other. Dad says he doesn't understand why girls have to shriek like that. There's
no way I can explain it to him.

Rachel must have grown another two inches
over the summer because when Mom hugged
her, Rachel was taller. She'll probably be the
tallest girl in seventh grade.

"I've never seen so many posters!" Rachel stood
in the middle of my room, shaking her head.
When she noticed Benjamin Moore she asked,
"How come that one's on your ceiling?"

"Lie down," I said.

"Not now."

"Yes, now . . ." I pushed her toward the bed. "It's the only way you can really see him."

Rachel shoved an armload of stuffed animals out of the way and lay down.

I flopped beside her. "Isn't he cute?"

"Yeah . . . he is."

"My mother calls him a hunk."

Rachel laughed.

"You know what I call him?"

"What?"

"Benjamin Moore."

"Benjamin Moore . . ." Rachel said, propping herself up on one elbow. "Isn't that a brand of paint?"

"Yes, but I love the name."

Rachel tossed a stuffed monkey at me. "You are so bizarre, Steph!"

I knew she meant that as a compliment.

"Is that the bee-sting necklace?" Rachel asked, reaching over to touch the locket around my neck. As she did, her hair, which is curly and reddish-brown, brushed against my arm. "Can I see how it works?"

"Sure."

I stepped on a bee in July while I was at Girl Scout camp and had an allergic reaction to its sting. The camp nurse had to revive me because I went into shock. The doctor said from now on I've got to carry pills with me in case I get stung again. They're small and blue. I hope I never have to take them. I'm not the greatest at swallowing pills. When I got back from camp, Gran Lola, my grandmother, gave me this necklace. I'd written all about it to Rachel.

I opened the small gold heart. "See . . ." I said, showing it to her, "instead of a place for a picture inside there's room for three pills."

Rachel touched them. "What did it feel like to be in shock?"

"I don't remember. I think I felt dizzy . . . then everything went black."

"Promise you'll always wear the necklace," Rachel said, "just in case."

"I promise."

"Good." She closed the heart. "Now . . . what about those cartons?" she asked, pointing across the room. "When are you going to unpack them?"

"Soon."

"I'll help you do it now."

"That's okay," I told her.

"You've got to get organized before school starts, Steph." She crossed the room and kneeled in front of the biggest carton. "Books!" she said. "You want to arrange them by subject or author?"

"This isn't a library," I said, "it's a bedroom."

"I know . . . but as long as we're doing it we might as well do it right."

"I don't need to have my books arranged in any special order," I said.

"But how will you find them?"

"I recognize them by their color."

Rachel laughed. "You're hopeless!"

Later, I walked Rachel home. It's funny, because when I first heard we were going to move I cried my eyes out. Then, when my parents told me we were moving to Palfrey's Pond, I couldn't believe how lucky I was, since that's where Rachel lives. Now, besides being best friends we'll also be neighbors. And moving just a few blocks away really isn't like moving at all. I think the only reason we moved is that our house needed a new roof and Mom and Dad just about passed out when they learned what it would cost.

The houses at Palfrey's Pond are scattered all around, not lined up in a row like on a regular street. They're supposed to look old, like the houses in a colonial village. Rachel's is on the other side of the pond. When we got there she said, "Now I'll walk *you* home."

I looked at her and we both laughed.

When we got back to my house I said, "Now I'll walk *you*."

Then Rachel walked me home.
Then I walked her.
Then she walked me.
We managed to walk each other home nine times before Mom called me inside.

Alison

The day before school started was hot and still. I was hanging out by the pond, dipping my feet into the water. That's when I first saw the girl. She was crouching by the tree with the big hole in it. I figured she was trying to get a look at the raccoon family that lives inside. I've never seen them myself, but my brother has.

I shook the water off my feet, put on my sandals, and walked over to her. She looked about Bruce's age. Her red and white striped T-shirt came down to her knees. Probably it belonged to her father. Her hair was long. She hadn't brushed it that day. I could tell by her crooked part and the tangles at the ends. I guess she wasn't worried about stepping on a bee because she was barefoot.

She had a small dog with her, the kind that has fur hanging over its eyes. As soon as I came close the dog started to bark.

"Be quiet, Maizie," the girl said. Then she turned to me. "Hi . . . I'm Alison. We just moved in. You probably didn't notice because we didn't have a moving van. We're renting Number 25."

"I'm Stephanie," I said. "I live here, too. Number 9."

Alison stood up and brushed off her hands. She reached under her T-shirt, into the pocket of her shorts, and pulled out a card. I was really surprised because I got one just like it last week. On the front it said, *Looking forward . . .* And inside it said, *to meeting you next Thursday*. It was signed *Natalie Remo, seventh grade homeroom teacher, Room 203*.

"What do you know about Mrs. Remo?" Alison asked. "Because that's who I've got for homeroom."

I guess she could tell I was surprised. She said, "You probably thought I was younger. Everyone does since I'm so small. But I'm going to be thirteen in April."

I didn't tell her I'd thought she was Bruce's age. Instead I said, "I'll be thirteen in February." I didn't mention the date either—February 2—

Ground Hog Day. "I'm in Mrs. Remo's home-room, too. She sent me the same card."

"Oh," Alison said. "I thought she sent it to me because I'm new. I'm from Los Angeles."

"My father's there now, on business," I told her. He's been there since the beginning of August, ever since we moved. I don't know how long he's going to be away this time. Once he had to go to Japan for six weeks.

Maizie, the dog, barked. Alison kneeled next to her. "What'd you say, Maizie?" she asked, pressing her ear right up to Maizie's mouth.

Maizie made a couple of sounds and Alison nodded, then giggled. "Oh, come on, Maizie," she said, as if she were talking to her dog. Then Alison looked up at me. "Maizie is such a char-acter! She told me to tell you she's glad we're in the same homeroom because she was worried about me not knowing anyone in my new school."

"Your dog told you that?"

"Yes," Alison said. "But look . . . I'd really appreciate it if you didn't say anything about it. Once people find out your dog can talk, forget it. In L.A. there were always reporters and photographers following us around. We're trying to avoid the same kind of publicity here."

"You mean," I said, "that your dog actually talks . . . like Mr. Ed, that talking horse who used to be on TV?"

"That horse didn't really talk," Alison said, as if I didn't know.

"Well," I said, scratching the mosquito bite on my leg, "exactly how does Maizie talk? I mean, does she talk in human words or what?"

"Of course she talks in words," Alison said. "But she doesn't speak perfect English because English isn't her first language. It's hard for a dog to learn other languages."

"What's her first language?" I asked.

"French."

"Oh," I said, "French." Now this was getting really good. "I'm taking Introduction to French this year."

"I'm taking Introduction to Spanish," Alison said. "I already speak French. I lived outside of Paris until I was six."

"I thought you were Chinese or something," I said.

"I'm Vietnamese," Alison said. "I'm adopted. My mother's American but she was married to Pierre Monceau when they adopted me. He's French. Mom came to the States after they got divorced. That's when she met Leon. He's my stepfather."

I absolutely love to hear the details of other peoples' lives! So I sat down beside Alison, hoping she would tell me more. Bruce says I'm nosey.

But that's not true. I've discovered, though, that you can't ask too many questions when you first meet people or they'll get the wrong idea. They may not understand that you're just very curious and accuse you of butting into their private business instead.

Alison fiddled with a twig, running it across Maizie's back. I didn't ask her any of the questions that were already forming in my mind. Instead I said, "Would your dog talk to me?"

"Maybe . . . if she's in the mood."

I cleared my throat. "Hi, Maizie," I said, as if I were talking to a little kid. "I'm your new neighbor, Stephanie Hirsch."

Maizie cocked her head at me as if she were actually listening. Her tiny bottom teeth stuck out, the opposite of mine. My top teeth stuck out before I got my braces. The orthodontist says I have an overbite. That would mean Maizie has an underbite.

"What kind of dog are you," I asked, patting her back. Her fur felt sticky, as if she'd been rolling in syrup.

"She's a mixture," Alison said. "We don't know anything about her parents so we don't know if they could talk or not. Probably not. Only one in seventeen million dogs can talk."

"One in seventeen million?"

"Yes. That's what the vet told us. It's extremely rare. Maizie is probably the only talking dog in all of Connecticut."

"Well," I said. "I can't wait for Rachel to meet Maizie."

"Who's Rachel?" Alison asked.

"She's my best friend."

"Oh, you have a best friend."

"She lives here, too. Number 16. She's really smart. She's never had less than an A in school." I stood up. "I have to go home now. But I'll see you tomorrow. The junior high bus stops in front of the lodge. That's the building down by the road. It's supposed to come at ten to eight."

"I know," Alison said. "I got a notice in the mail." She stood up too. "Do you wear jeans or skirts to school here?"

"Either," I said.

"What about shoes?"

I looked at Alison's bare feet. "Yes," I said, "you have to wear them."

"I mean what *kind* of shoes . . . running shoes or sandals or what?"

"Most of the kids here wear topsiders."

"Topsiders are so preppy," Alison said.

"You don't *have* to wear them," I told her. "You can wear whatever you want."

"Good," Alison said. "I will."

Rachel's Room

"Dogs can't talk," Rachel said that night, when I told her about Alison and Maizie.

I was sitting on Rachel's bed. Her cats, Burt and Harry, were nestled against my legs, purring. They're named after some beer commercial from Rachel's parents' youth.

Rachel was going through her closet, pulling out clothes that don't fit anymore. In her closet everything faces the same way and hangs on white plastic hangers.

In my closet nothing is in order. Last year Rachel tried to organize it for me. But a week later it was all a mess again and she was disappointed.

"Are you giving away your Yale sweatshirt?" I asked.

"No, that still fits."

"What about your red plaid shirt?"

"Yes . . . do you want it?"

"I'll try it on and see," I said.

Rachel took it off a hanger and handed it to me. "I've got to do some back-to-school shopping."

I did mine last week. I got a skirt, a couple of shirts, a sweater and a pair of designer jeans. Rachel's mother says designer jeans are an incredible rip-off and she won't let Rachel or her sixteen-year-old sister, Jessica, buy them. Rachel also has a brother, Charles. He's fifteen. He doesn't get along with the rest of the family so he goes away to school. I doubt that he cares about designer jeans.

My mother says she admires Mrs. Robinson. "Nell Robinson sticks to her guns," is how Mom puts it. "I wish I had such strong convictions." But she doesn't. That's how come I got a pair of *Guess* jeans. It's not that I care about labels. It's just that I like the way they fit.

I pulled my T-shirt over my head.

"Steph!" Rachel cried, lowering the window shades. "I wish you'd remember you're going into junior high. You can't run around like a baby anymore. Where's your bra?"

"At home. It was too hot to wear it."

I tried on Rachel's red plaid shirt. It's made of flannel that's been washed so many times it's almost as thin as regular cotton. It felt soft against my skin. I buttoned it and rolled up the sleeves. Then I jumped off the bed, waking Burt, who yawned and stretched. I looked at myself in Rachel's mirror. "I like it," I said.

"It's yours," Rachel told me.

"Thanks." I took the shirt off. Even though the shades were down the breeze from the window felt cool against my skin.

"Put your T-shirt on, Steph," Rachel said, tossing it to me, then turning away.

I slipped it on and flopped back onto Rachel's bed. Burt was chasing a rubber band around on the floor. Harry was still curled in a ball, fast asleep.

Rachel went to her desk. She held up her notebook. It was covered in wallpaper. I recognized the pattern—tiny dots and flowers in pink and green—from their bathroom. It looked great. "Do you have any extra?"

"I think we have some blue stripes left from the dining room. Want me to take a look?"

"Sure."

I followed Rachel into the hall. She opened the stepladder in the closet and climbed to the top. "Here it is," she said, handing me the roll.

Then we went downstairs. Mrs. Robinson was at the dining room table with stacks of papers and books spread out in front of her. She's a trial lawyer. "Stephanie . . ." she said, glancing up for a minute, "good to see you!"

"Mom's got a big case starting tomorrow," Rachel explained.

Mrs. Robinson is always either starting a big case or in the middle of one.

Mr. Robinson was at the kitchen table, also surrounded by books and papers. He teaches history at the high school. As we walked through the kitchen he popped two Pepto Bismol tablets into his mouth. "I always get nervous before school starts," he said, chewing them. "You'd think by now I'd be used to it, but I'm not."

"I never knew teachers get nervous about starting school," I said.

Mr. Robinson nodded. "It starts in my stomach in August and doesn't let up until the end of September." The Pepto Bismol made his teeth look pink.

"I'm going over to Steph's," Rachel said. "I'll be back in less than an hour."

"Okay," Mr. Robinson said.

Rachel carried the wallpaper. As we passed Number 25 I said, "That's Alison's house. She's in Mrs. Remo's homeroom, too."

Rachel froze. "That is so unfair!" She has someone named Ms. Levano for homeroom. "I don't know what I'm going to do if we're not in the same classes."

"Don't worry," I said, "we will be."

"I hope you're right."

The lights were on in Alison's house but the curtains were pulled closed so we couldn't see anything.

"What's she like?" Rachel asked.

"She's small and friendly," I said. "She seems okay."

"Except for that talking-dog business."

"It *is* possible," I said.

"Come on, Stephanie! There's no such thing as a talking dog. If there was we'd have heard about it."

"Maybe so," I said.

When we got to my house Mom was working at her computer. Since she got it she doesn't have to spend such long hours at the office. "Dad called, Steph. He's waiting for you to call him back."

"Okay . . ." I left Rachel in the den with Mom and called Dad from the kitchen phone. It's funny talking to him in L.A. because when it's eight o'clock here it's only five o'clock there. He was still at the office and I was about to get ready for bed.

"I miss you," Dad said.

"I miss you, too. When will you be home?"

"I'm not sure yet."

"I hope it won't be long."

"I'll definitely be home for Thanksgiving."

"Dad . . . that's more than two months away."

"There's no way I can get back before then, Steph. I have to make two trips to Hawaii and one to the Orient."

I didn't say anything for a minute. Neither did Dad. Then he said, "Well . . . have a good first day at school."

"Rachel and I aren't even in the same homeroom," I said.

"Don't worry . . . you'll do fine without Rachel."

"I'm not worried. Who said I was worried? I'm just saying it's not fair since we're best friends."

"You and Rachel will still see each other after school."

"What do you mean *after* school?" I asked. "We'll be on the same bus and we'll probably be in all the same classes."

"So you'll be together all the time . . . just like before."

"That's right," I said.

"What's the weather like?" Dad asked. He loves to hear about the weather.

"Hot and humid with a chance of thunderstorms."

We talked for a few more minutes, then I went back to the den.

"Rachel's waiting upstairs," Mom told me.

"Surprise!" Rachel called, when I got to my room. She held up my notebook. She had covered it while I was talking to Dad. "What do you think?" she asked.

I wanted to cover my own notebook is what I thought. But I couldn't say that to Rachel. Her feelings would be hurt. So I said, "It looks good."

"It's really hard to get perfect corners with wallpaper," she said. "Want me to print your name and address inside?"

"I'll do it myself."

"Okay . . . but I'll draw the lines so the letters are even." She searched my desk. "Where's your ruler?" she asked.

"Don't worry about it," I said. "I'll do it later."

When Rachel left I took a bath and washed my hair. It feels funny washing short hair when you're used to having it longer. The other night, when Rachel first saw me, she'd asked, "What'd you do to your hair, Steph?"

"I got carried away," I'd told her. "It was so hot when I came home from camp I decided to cut it all off."

"Yourself?"

"No, I went to the Final Cut."

"It's kind of interesting," Rachel had said. "Especially from the back."

I liked my short hair for about a week. Now I wish I'd never done it. It'll probably take all year to grow back.

I wrapped myself in a towel and left the steamy bathroom. I still couldn't believe Dad wasn't coming home until Thanksgiving. He's never been away that long. But fall goes a lot faster than winter, I reminded myself. It's my favorite time of year, not counting spring. I also like summer a lot. And winter is fun because of the snow . . . I began to feel better.

Before I got into bed I found my ruler. It was under Wiley Coyote, my number one stuffed animal. Dad won him for me last year at the Jaycees' Carnival. I drew four straight lines on the inside of my notebook, then printed my name and address. There, I thought, admiring my work.

I got into bed and looked up at Benjamin Moore. I hope I meet someone just like him at junior high.

Homeroom

I introduced Alison to Rachel at the bus stop the next morning. Alison was wearing baggy pants, a white shirt about ten sizes too big, and running shoes. She had sunglasses around her neck, on a leash, and a canvas bag slung over her shoulder. The tangles were brushed out of her hair but her part was still crooked. All in all she looked great.

Then Rachel introduced us to Dana Carpenter, a ninth grader who also lives at Palfrey's Pond. I was glad we'd have company riding the bus because I'd heard rumors that some people like to give seventh graders a hard time on their first day at junior high.

When the bus came Rachel and I found two

seats together. Alison sat two rows ahead of us with Dana Carpenter. Nobody seemed interested in giving us a hard time.

"You didn't tell me Alison's Chinese," Rachel whispered when the bus got going.

"She's Vietnamese," I told Rachel. "She's adopted."

"Oh," Rachel said. "She doesn't even seem scared."

"I don't think she's the type to get scared over school," I said.

"I wish I weren't," Rachel said. "I couldn't eat a thing this morning. I was shaking so bad I could hardly brush my teeth."

I tried to help Rachel calm down by offering her a chocolate chip cookie from my lunch bag. She nibbled at it, then handed it back to me. No point in wasting it, I thought, so I finished it myself.

At the next bus stop six kids got on the bus and one of them was the best looking boy I have ever seen in person in my whole life. He looked almost as good as Benjamin Moore.

"Hey, Jeremy!" a group of boys called. "Back here . . ."

The boy, Jeremy, walked right by me on his way to the back of the bus. As he did his arm brushed against my shoulder. I turned around to get a better look at him. So did Rachel. So did most of the girls on the bus. He had brown hair, brown eyes, a great smile and he wore a chartreuse colored jacket. I learned that color from my deluxe Crayola crayon box when I was in third grade. On the back of his jacket it said *Dragons* and under that, *1962*.

"He has a great body," Rachel whispered to me.

"Yeah," I said. "He's a real hunk." We started to laugh and I could feel Rachel relax, until the bus pulled up to school. Then she stiffened. But her homeroom, 7-202, turned out to be right next to mine, 7-203.

"Stay with me until the bell rings," she begged. "And promise that you'll meet me here, in the hall, before first class so we can compare schedules . . . okay?"

"Okay," I said. Alison was standing next to me. She kept putting her sunglasses on, then taking them off again.

"Look," I said to Rachel, "there go the Klaff twins. Kara's in your homeroom and Peter's in mine." The Klaff twins were in our sixth grade class. Their mother is our doctor. I figured Rachel would feel better knowing that Kara's in her homeroom.

"Well . . . I guess this is it," Rachel said. "I'm going to count to ten, then I'm going to go in."

"Okay."

She counted very slowly. When she got to ten she said, "If I live through this I'll see you later." She turned and marched into her homeroom. Sometimes Rachel is really dramatic.

Alison and I found desks next to each other. As soon as I sat down Eric Macaulay yelled, "Hey . . . it's Hershey Bar!" He *would* have to be in my homeroom! Last year he and some other boys got the brilliant idea of calling me Hershey Bar just because my last name is Hirsch. They're so stupid! Of course Eric had to go and take the desk right in front of mine.

Besides Eric Macaulay and Peter Klaff there were two other boys and two girls from sixth grade in my homeroom. One of them, Amber Ackbourne, I have never liked. She has such an attitude! The other one, Miri Levine, is okay. She took the desk on the other side of mine. I set my notebook, covered in Rachel's dining room wallpaper, on my desk. Miri Levine looked at it and said, "I like your notebook."

I said, "Thanks."

She had a plain spiral notebook on her desk.

"How'd you get the corners so perfect?" she asked.

"Rachel covered it for me."

"Oh, Rachel . . . everything she does is perfect."

"I know," I said.

Alison unpacked her canvas bag. She pulled

out a gray-blue stone, a roll of Scotch tape, a pad decorated with stickers, a Uniball pen, cherry flavored lip gloss and a small framed photo. Then she put everything back into her bag except the stone. She passed it to me. "It's my favorite," she said.

The stone was smooth and warm from Alison's hand.

When the bell rang a woman walked into our room. I was really surprised when she said, "Good morning, class. I'm Natalie Remo, your home-room teacher."

I'd expected someone young, around twenty-four, with short brown hair . . . someone a little overweight, like me. But Mrs. Remo was about my mother's age, which is thirty-eight, and she's black. She was wearing a suit. I noticed when she took off her jacket that the lining matched her blouse. She also had on gold earrings which she pulled off and set on her desk.

"Still pretty warm out," she said, fanning herself with a yellow pad. "More like summer than fall." She walked around the room opening the windows. "There . . . that's better." She stood in front of the class again. "I hope you all received my cards."

No one said anything.

"Did you . . . receive my cards?"

Everyone mumbled, "Yes."

"Good," Mrs. Remo said. "Welcome to J. E. Fox Junior High."

I happen to know that our school is named for John Edward Fox. He was supposed to be the first principal here but he died right before the school opened.

"I teach math," Mrs. Remo said. "So eventually most of you will wind up in one of my classes."

Nobody said anything.

"Well . . ." Mrs. Remo continued, "either you're all still asleep or you're feeling pretty unsure about junior high. I think by the end of the day you're going to feel much better. Once you get used to changing classes you'll all relax."

Nobody said anything.

Mrs. Remo smiled at us. "All right . . . let's see who's here today." She called our names in alphabetical order. Amber Ackbourne was first. She always is.

When Mrs. Remo called my name I raised my hand and said, "Here . . ." As I did, Eric Macaulay turned around and whispered, "Hershey Bar." I tried to kick him but I missed and kicked the leg of the chair instead. I hurt my foot so bad I groaned.

"Yes, Stephanie? Did you have something to say?" Mrs. Remo asked.

"No," I said, and Eric Macaulay laughed.

When she got to Alison Mrs. Remo pronounced her last name Mon See U.

Alison corrected her. "It's spelled M-o-n-c-e-a-u," she said. "But it's pronounced Mon So. It's French."

"Of course," Mrs. Remo said. "I should have known."

Everyone turned and looked at Alison. Alison just sat there as if she didn't notice but I could see her clutching her favorite stone.

After that we got our locker assignments and our class schedules. Then Mrs. Remo told us when the bell rang we should proceed to our first class in an orderly way. We waited for the bell, then we all jumped up and raced for the door.

"Orderly . . ." Mrs. Remo reminded us.

Rachel was already in the hall, waiting. "Well," she said, "let's see your schedule."

I handed it to her. I knew from the expression on her face that the news wasn't good before she said, "I can't believe this. We don't have one class together. Not one!"

"Let me see," I said, reaching for her schedule and mine. I compared them. "Look at this," I said. "We both have first lunch period. And we're in the same gym class."

"Gym," Rachel sniffed. "Big deal."

I felt bad for Rachel because Alison, Miri Levine and I are in the same English, math and social studies classes. Rachel has math first period, with Mrs. Remo. I said, "You're lucky. She's nice."

"Out of my way, Hershey Bar!" Eric Macaulay said, shoving me.

"Watch it," I told him.

"Watch it yourself," he said. "I've got to get to my math class. If I can only find room 203."

"This *is* room 203," Alison told him.

He looked up at the number on the door. "Hey, you're right. I've got math right here. Right in my own homeroom."

"Oh no!" Rachel groaned. "I'm in *his* math class. It couldn't be worse."

"Yes it could," I told her.

"You know your problem, Stephanie?" Rachel said.

"No, what?"

"You're an eternal optimist!"

"What's an optimist?"

"Look it up!"

As soon as I got to English class I looked up optimist in the dictionary. *Optimist: One who has a disposition or tendency to look on the more favorable side of happenings and to anticipate the most favorable result.* Well, I thought, what's wrong with that?

6

Maizie's Story

That afternoon, on our way to the school bus, Rachel admitted school hadn't been that bad. She knew some kids in her classes from last year and one, Stacey Green, she knew from music camp.

"You see? I told you it would all work out. The Eternal Optimist strikes again."

Rachel raised her eyebrows at me.

" 'Optimist'," I said, " *'one who has a tendency to look on the more favorable side of happenings'*."

"I'm impressed," Rachel said.

The boy in the chartreuse dragon jacket sat behind us on the bus. I heard him say something about a left wing to the boy next to him. I wasn't sure if he was talking about a bird or a plane.

When we got off the bus Alison asked us both to come over to her house.

Rachel said, "I have a flute lesson at four-thirty."

"You play the flute?" Alison asked.

"Yes," Rachel said.

"Are you any good?" Alison asked.

I laughed. Alison didn't know yet that Rachel is good at everything. "She's practically a professional," I told Alison.

"I'm not *that* good," Rachel said.

Alison checked her watch. "Look, it's only three-thirty . . . so why don't you come over for a little while? My dog can talk."

Rachel glanced at me. I wasn't supposed to have told anyone about Maizie so I hoped she wouldn't give me away.

"Your dog can talk?" Rachel asked.

"Uh huh," Alison said.

"Well . . ." Rachel said, "I guess I could come over for a little while."

Maizie met us at Alison's kitchen door, shaking her little rear end from side to side, then leaping into the air. Alison put her books on the kitchen table and scooped Maizie up into her arms. She put her face right up close to Maizie's. It looked like they were talking—in French, I think. It was hard to tell because Alison spoke very softly. But

Maizie nodded, made small sounds and sometimes let out a bark.

Rachel looked skeptical as she watched the two of them. I learned that word—skeptical—from her. It means to question or doubt.

"What's new with Maizie?" I asked Alison.

Alison put Maizie down and giggled. "She told me the silliest story."

"What story?" Rachel asked.

"I'm not sure it's true," Alison said as she poured three glasses of grape juice and set a box of pretzels on the table.

"Tell it to us anyway," Rachel said, taking a handful of pretzels.

"Well . . ." Alison began. She told us this story about her stepfather, Leon, who took Maizie for a walk in the woods. While they were walking Leon tripped over a branch and fell into the brook. He got soaked, which Maizie thought was a big joke.

"That's the whole story?" Rachel asked.

"Yes." Alison looked at me. "Of course, Maizie might have made it up. Sometimes when she's bored she sits around making up stories."

Rachel still wasn't convinced and Alison could tell. "I suppose we could ask Leon if it's true," she said.

Alison pressed the button on the intercom.

Every house in Palfrey's Pond has an intercom. Ours doesn't work but probably when Dad comes home he'll fix it.

"Hi, Leon . . ." Alison said. "I'm home."

"Be right down," a man's voice answered.

In a minute Leon came down the stairs and into the kitchen. He was tall and mostly bald.

"Hello, Pumpkin," Leon said to Alison, ruffling her hair.

Pumpkin? I thought.

"This is my stepfather, Leon Wishnik," Alison said, introducing us.

Leon smiled. He had very nice teeth. I notice everybody's teeth. Mom says it's because I wear braces. She says once they come off I won't be so interested in teeth. But Dad says my interest in teeth could mean that I want to be a dentist.

"Glad to meet you, Rachel," Leon said to me.

"I'm Stephanie," I told him.

He laughed. "Well, glad to meet *you*, Stephanie. And glad to meet you, too, Rachel." Leon lifted the lid off the pot on the stove and stirred. It smelled great.

"Maizie told me about your walk," Alison said to Leon. "Is it true . . . did you really trip and fall into the brook?"

Leon turned away from the stove and wagged his finger at Maizie. "I asked you not to tell anyone about that," he said to her.

Maizie ran under the kitchen table to hide.

"Then it's true?" Alison asked.

"Yes," Leon said. "My shoes will never be the same."

"Are you saying that your dog *really* talks?" Rachel asked Leon. I stared at her. She'd lowered her voice by an octave and sounded exactly like her mother. I could tell Leon was impressed. Tonight, while they were eating dinner, he would probably say to Alison, *That Rachel . . . she's certainly mature for her age.* He wouldn't know that this morning she was shaking with fear over the idea of junior high.

"Yes," Leon said, sighing, "Maizie talks . . . usually too much." He rested the wooden spoon on a saucer. "I've got to get back to work now. Nice to meet you, Stephanie and Rachel."

"Nice to meet you, too," we said.

Rachel still had a handful of pretzels and was licking the salt off them one at a time. She always licks pretzels until they're soggy.

Alison asked if we wanted to see her room. "But I'm warning you . . . it's incredibly ugly."

"So what'd you think?" I asked Rachel, as I walked her home from Alison's house.

"Obviously she's very insecure," Rachel said. "That's why she uses that talking dog story."

"But Maizie *can* talk," I said. "You heard what Leon said."

"You're so gullible, Steph!" Rachel said. "But I suppose that's part of your charm."

I had no idea what gullible meant and I wasn't about to ask so I just nodded and said, "It runs in my family."

Rachel gave me one of her skeptical looks, then said, "Well . . . I think we should try to help her get adjusted here. I think we should try to be her friends."

"I think so, too," I said.

7

Bruce

Bruce's fifth grade teacher is Mrs. Stein. I also had her. But she taught fourth grade then. "She remembers you, Steph . . ." Bruce said at breakfast the following Friday. "She said you came in second in the reading contest." He reached across the table for the box of Cheerios.

"Rachel came in first," I told him, as I buttered my toast. I like my toast very dark. I try to catch it just before it burns and is ruined.

"Mrs. Stein says she remembers Rachel, too," Bruce said.

"Rachel's teachers always remember her," I said. In fourth grade Rachel started reading the kinds of books her sister, Jessica, was reading for eighth grade English. When we gave book talks in class Rachel never reported on those books, though. She'd choose a book she thought a normal fourth grader would like instead.

By sixth grade everybody knew Rachel was smart but she didn't like it if the teacher made a big thing out of it. During math she'd go around helping kids who didn't understand. Our sixth grade teacher called Rachel his teaching assistant.

I was still sitting at the kitchen table, finishing my toast and thinking about Rachel, when Mom opened a kitchen drawer and said, "Oh, no!"

"Did you get a mouse?" I asked.

Mom slammed the drawer. "I give up!" she said. "They ate the peanut butter right off the traps. I'm going to have to call Mr. Kravitz."

"Who's he?" Bruce asked.

"The exterminator," Mom said. "He's the one who bought the yellow house from us."

"I never knew we sold our house to an exterminator," I said. "I thought Mr. and Mrs. Kravitz owned a shoe store."

Mom laughed. "Where did you get that idea?"

"I don't know."

"Well, Mr. Kravitz is an exterminator," Mom said.

That night Aunt Denise asked Mom to go to the movies with her. Besides being sisters, Mom and Aunt Denise are also best friends. I wish I had a sister, even though Rachel says she and Jessica don't get along that well. Mom has two sisters, Robin and Denise. Mom is the middle one. Her name is Rowena.

"Maybe I should call Mrs. Greco," Mom said at dinner.

"I'm too old for a sitter," I told her. Mrs. Greco sat for us when we lived in the yellow house. "I could be a sitter myself."

"You're not too old for companionship," Mom said.

"I have Bruce."

Bruce smiled. "She has me," he said, as if it were his idea. "And the mice."

"Very funny." Mom poured her tea. She took a few sips, then said, "Tell you what . . . if I'm going to be home by midnight you two can stay by yourselves . . . that is, if it works out tonight. But if I'm staying out later than that, you'll have a companion."

"You mean someone like Rachel?" I asked. "That kind of companion?"

"We'll see," Mom said.

We'll see is what Mom says when she wants to change the subject.

As soon as Mom left I took the phone into the pantry and called Rachel. The pantry is small, like a closet, but it's the only place in this house where I can talk on the phone in private. There's a light inside and enough room to sit on the floor, as long as I don't try to stretch out my legs. There's a nice spicy smell, too, which makes me hungry, even if I've just finished dinner.

While I was talking to Rachel I munched on the macadamia peanut brittle one of Mom's clients brought her from Hawaii. I tried Alison's number after I'd talked to Rachel, but her line was busy so I went into the den to watch TV with Bruce.

Next year, when we get cable, we'll have MTV. Aunt Denise's neighborhood already has cable, and my cousin, Howard, watches MTV all the time, even while he's doing his homework. Mom says I'll never be allowed to do my homework in front of the tube. I say, *We'll see.*

Bruce went to bed at ten. One thing about Bruce, he falls asleep really fast, as soon as his head hits the pillow. Same as me.

I went to the bathroom and used the Water Pik. Then I scrubbed my face. Some nights I don't bother washing my face at all. I keep forgetting to ask Mom if scrubbing your face will keep you from getting acne. I scrubbed mine until it turned very pink, to make up for all the nights I'm too lazy to do anything.

Next, I decided to call Dad. I went down the hall to Mom's room and looked up Dad's number in the little phone book she keeps in her night table. There was also a flashlight in her drawer, and some lip goo.

I dialed the number of Dad's apartment. The phone rang three times before Dad's answering machine clicked on with Dad's voice saying, "This is Steve Hirsch. I'm not home right now but if you leave a message . . ."

"Hi Dad," I said at the sound of the beep. "It's Stephanie. I just wanted to say hello."

I went back to my room. The house was so quiet. There was a half moon outside my window and it lit up Benjamin Moore's poster. Well, Benjamin, I thought, as I got into bed. It's just you and me tonight. I wish you were real. I wish you could come down off the ceiling and kiss me goodnight. You look like you'd be a great kisser.

I rolled over and fell asleep. I slept until a frightening sound woke me. I sat up in bed, my heart pounding. Then I raced down the hall to Mom's room. But Mom wasn't home yet. I grabbed the baseball bat from under her bed. She keeps it there when Dad is away, just in case. I glanced at the clock—11:20—not even an hour since I'd gone to bed. I listened for other sounds, trying to decide if I should call the police or a neighbor, but all I heard was Bruce, crying and calling for Mom. I ran to his room, clutching the baseball bat, and that's when I realized nothing was wrong in the house. It was just Bruce, having one of his nightmares.

I sat down at the edge of his bed. He threw his arms around me, sobbing. I held him tight. I would never put my arms around him during the day. Not that he'd let me. His face felt hot and wet with tears. He smelled like a puppy.

"The usual?" I asked.

"Yes . . . I saw it," he said, gulping for air. "I saw the bomb . . . it was silver . . . shaped like a football . . . rolling around in the sky. When it got to our house it started to fall . . . straight down . . . and then there was a flash of light . . . and I heard the explosion . . ."

"It's all right," I told him. "It was just a bad dream."

"It's coming," Bruce said, "the bomb is coming. . . ."

"But it's not coming tonight," I told him, stroking his hair. His hair was soft and damp around the edges.

"How do you know?"

"I just know. So there's no point in worrying about it now."

"It could be the end of the world," Bruce said, shuddering.

"Look," I told him, "if it happens, it happens." I don't like to think about the end of the world or the bomb so I don't. I'm good at putting bad things out of my mind. That's why I'm an optimist.

I lay down on Bruce's bed and held him until he fell back asleep. The good thing about his nightmares is that he never has more than one a night. It's as if he just needs to be reassured that the end of the world isn't coming yet.

I guess I fell asleep holding Bruce because soon my mother was gently shaking me and whispering, "Come on, Steph . . . let's go back to bed."

She walked me down the hall to my room. "He had a nightmare," I said, groggily.

Mom tucked me into bed and kissed both my cheeks.

The next morning, when I came into the kitchen, Bruce was sitting at the table, writing a letter.

I poured myself a glass of orange juice. "Who are you writing to today?" I asked.

"The President," Bruce said.

"Oh, the President." I set out a bowl for my cereal.

"You should write, too," Bruce said. "If everybody writes to the President he'll have to listen. Here . . ." Bruce shoved a piece of notebook paper at me.

"Not while I'm eating," I said. I finished my cereal, rinsed the bowl, then brought the box of doughnuts to the table. Mom is a doughnut addict but since we moved she's buying only the plain or the whole wheat kind. No artificial flavors or colors, no preservatives. Mom will eat only one a day now, at the most two, because she's trying to lose weight. I miss glazed doughnuts. I miss chocolate and jelly filled too.

"Mom is going to kill you," Bruce said.

"For what?"

"Polishing off three doughnuts."

Three? I counted the ones left in the box. He was right. Sometimes when I'm eating I forget to keep track.

I washed my doughnuts down with another glass of juice and then I started my letter.

Dear Mr. President,

I really think you should do more to make sure we never have a nuclear war. War is stupid, as you know. My brother, who is ten, has nightmares about it. Probably other kids do, too. I have mainly good dreams. My friend, Rachel, says I am an optimist. Even so, I don't want to die and neither do any of my friends. Why can't you arrange more meetings with other countries and try harder to get along. Make some treaties. Make them for one hundred years so we don't have to worry for a long time. You could also get rid of all the nuclear weapons in the world and then maybe Bruce, my brother, could get a decent night's sleep.

Yours truly,
Stephanie B. Hirsch

I like using my middle initial for formal occasions. The *B* stands for Behrens. That's my mother's maiden name.

I shoved my letter across the table, at Bruce. He read it. "This is about dreams," he said.

"No, it's not," I told him. "It's about nuclear war."

"But there's a lot in it about dreams."

"So . . . what's wrong with that? If *you* didn't have bad dreams about nuclear war we wouldn't be writing to the President, would we?"

"I don't know," Bruce said. "And you didn't make paragraphs, either."

"I didn't make paragraphs on purpose," I said. That wasn't true but I wasn't going to admit it to Bruce. "I think it's an outstanding letter," I said. "I think the part about the hundred year treaties is really brilliant."

"In a hundred years we'll be dead," Bruce said, sounding gloomy.

"So will everybody."

"No . . . people who aren't born yet won't be."

"That doesn't count," I said. "Everybody we know will be dead in a hundred years."

"I don't like to think about being dead," Bruce said.

"Who does?" I passed him the doughnut box. "Here," I said, "have one . . . it'll make you feel better."

"I don't like these doughnuts," he said, "especially in the morning."

8

Saturdays

Ever since Dad went to L.A. Mom takes Bruce and me to the office with her on Saturdays. She's got a travel agency in town. Going Places is the name of it. Aunt Denise says Mom is a real go-getter. She says she hopes I take after her. I don't know if I do or not. Mom had puppy fat like me when she was a girl. And we both have brown hair and blue eyes if that means anything.

I reminded Mom this was the Saturday Rachel and I were going to shop with Alison, to help her fix up her room. "Rachel says it's very depressing the way it is. It's all gray."

"Gray is a sophisticated color," Mom said.

"But it's so blah . . . it doesn't suit Alison," I told her. "Alison is a very cheerful person."

"She sounds like a good match for you," Mom said.

"I think she is. I think we're really going to get along."

"What about Rachel?" Mom asked.

"She wants to be Alison's friend, too. She wants to help her get adjusted here. We're meeting in front of the bank at one o'clock. Is that okay?"

"I think we can arrange to give you the afternoon off," Mom said. "But try and get as much as you can done this morning."

"You know I'm a hard worker," I said.

My job is filing. Craig taught me how to do it. He's one of Mom's part-time assistants. He wears a gold earring in one ear and has a scraggly moustache that he's always touching to make sure it's still there. He wants to write travel guides to places like Africa and India when he's out of college. So far he's only been as far away as Maine.

There's no big deal to filing as long as you know the alphabet. The only thing I have to remember is that we file front to back here, which means I have to put the latest papers at the end of the folder, not at the beginning.

While I was filing, who should come into Going Places but Jeremy Dragon, that good-looking boy from the bus. Only Rachel and Alison know my secret name for him. I named him that because of his chartreuse jacket with the dragon on the back. He wears it every day. He was with two of his friends. I recognized them from the bus, too.

"Can I help you?" Craig asked them.

"We need some brochures," Jeremy Dragon said, "for a school project."

"Help yourself," Craig said.

"How many can we take?" one of Jeremy's friends asked.

I came running up front then. "How about five apiece?" I said.

Jeremy and his two friends looked at me. So did Craig.

"Aren't you supposed to be filing?" Craig asked.

"In a minute," I told him and hoped that he would go do something else. When he still didn't get the hint I said, "*I'll* take care of this, Craig." I've heard Mom say that to him lots of times.

Finally Craig got the message and said, "Oh . . ." and he excused himself to go back to the desk where he'd been working.

"You should try the Ivory Coast," I said to Jeremy, handing him a brochure. "And Thailand . . . that's a good one." I handed him that brochure, too. "I also recommend Alaska . . . and then there's Brazil." Each time I handed Jeremy Dragon a brochure our fingers touched and I got a tingly feeling up my arm.

"We're doing a project on marketing and advertising," Jeremy said, "not on travel."

"Oh," I said, as his friends helped themselves to more than five brochures apiece. Then I quickly added, "If you ever do want to plan a trip this is the best travel agency in town. My mother owns it so I should know."

"We'll keep that in mind," Jeremy said. He kind of waved as he went out the door.

"My name is Stephanie," I called after him. But he didn't hear me.

I couldn't wait to tell Rachel and Alison about my morning.

9

Gena Farrell

Here's what we bought for Alison's room: two lamp shades, one comforter, a set of flowered sheets, four throw pillows, three posters and one box of push pins.

We shopped all over town, walking from store to store, until my feet ached. Rachel said it was important to see everything available before making a decision. She took notes on what we saw, and where. I hoped we'd run into Jeremy Dragon again but we didn't. Eventually we wound up where we started, at Bed and Bath. I couldn't believe how Alison just bought whatever she wanted. Even though the sheets and the throw pillows were on sale, they were still very expensive. Alison charged everything on her mother's American Express card.

"You mean she just gave you her credit card . . ." I asked, "just like that?"

"She trusts me," Alison said.

"I know, but still . . ." I said. "Did she tell you how much you could spend?"

"We talked about what I needed," Alison said.

"At least you got some of it on sale," Rachel said. "My mother buys everything on sale. And you got very good things. It pays to buy the best because it lasts longer."

I don't necessarily agree with that. Take my flowered sweatshirt. If I had bought the expensive kind I'd be stuck with it as long as it fit. But I bought the rip-off sweatshirt which only cost half as much so when it fell apart in the wash after a couple of months I didn't mind.

"Let's meet tomorrow morning at my house," Alison said, "around eleven. And you guys can help me fix up my room . . . okay?"

"Sure," I said.

"I'm going to visit my grandmother in the morning," Rachel said, "but I should be back around noon."

Rachel's grandmother had a stroke last spring. Once, I went with her family to the nursing home, but I got really upset because Rachel's grandmother couldn't walk or talk. Rachel says her grandmother understands everything they say and someday she may even be able to speak again. I don't know. I hope that never happens to Gran Lola or Papa Jack. It would be too sad.

On Sunday morning I got to Alison's house right on the dot of eleven. I rang the bell and a woman opened the door. She was wearing jeans and that red and white T-shirt Alison had been wearing on the day that we met. She looked very familiar.

"Hello," she said, "I'm Alison's mother. Are you Stephanie?"

"Yes."

"Alison's in her room. You can go on up . . ."

I started up the stairs. Then Alison's mother called, "Thanks for helping Alison find such beautiful things yesterday."

I stopped and turned at the landing, looking down at her. I know who she looks like, I thought. She looks like Gena Farrell, the TV star.

I went to Alison's room. She was unrolling her posters and laying them out on the floor. "Hi," I said. Maizie was on the bed. She barked at me. "Hello, Maizie." As soon as I spoke she turned her back. I guess she wasn't interested in having a conversation.

"Your mother looks a lot like Gena Farrell," I told Alison.

"I know," Alison said.

"I guess everybody tells her that."

"Yes. Especially since she is Gena Farrell."

"Your mother *is* Gena Farrell, the TV star?"

"She's an actress," Alison said, "not a TV star." She held a poster of Bruce Springsteen against the wall. "What do you think?"

"I can't believe this!" I said. "Your mother is Gena Farrell and you never said anything?"

"What should I have said?" Alison asked, holding up a second poster. This one showed a gorilla lying on a sofa. "Do you like it here or do you think I should hang it over my desk?"

"Over your desk," I said. "I just can't believe that you didn't tell us!"

"Would it have made a difference?" Alison put the posters on her bed.

"No," I said, "but . . ."

"But what?" Now she looked directly at me, waiting for me to say something.

"Nothing . . ."

"Get down, Maizie!" Alison shooed her off the bed.

Maizie growled.

"She can't stand it when people gush over my mother," Alison said. "She'll try to bite anyone who does. You wouldn't believe how many times she's tried to bite reporters."

"Really?"

"Yes," Alison said, taking the comforter out of its plastic bag. "Give me a hand getting this on the bed."

The comforter had tiny rosebuds all over it. And the lamp shades, which had been my idea, were made of the same fabric. Rachel said the lamp shades were unnecessary and too expensive, but Alison bought them anyway. At the time I thought it was to please me, since everything else had been Rachel's idea. But now that I knew Alison's mother was Gena Farrell I wasn't so sure. I mean, Gena Farrell is famous! She must be very rich.

I helped Alison hang her posters. I wished I had thought of push pins when I was hanging mine. They don't take the paint off the wall and they make such tiny holes that no one would ever notice them.

When we'd finished Alison said, "Do you know how to play Spit?"

"Spit as in saliva?" I asked.

Alison laughed. "Spit as in the card game."

"There's a card game called Spit?"

"Yes." Alison opened her desk drawer and took out a deck of cards. She shuffled, divided them into two piles, then explained the rules of the game.

By the time Rachel got there Alison and I were in the middle of a really fast hand and couldn't stop laughing. "We're playing Spit," I told Rachel.

"What?" Rachel said.

"It's a card game."

"You want me to teach you?" Alison asked Rachel.

"No . . ." Rachel said. "I came over to help with your room but I see it's all done."

Alison collected the cards and wrapped a rubber band around them.

"Doesn't it look great?" I asked Rachel.

"Actually, it does," Rachel said. "It looks just like a flower garden. Maybe I should be an interior designer."

"Did you recognize Alison's mother?" I asked Rachel.

"No, should I have?" Rachel asked.

"She's Gena Farrell," I said.

Maizie began to bark.

"Who's Gena Farrell?"

"Alison's mother!"

"I got that part," Rachel said. "The part I didn't get is *who* is Gena Farrell?"

"The TV star," I said.

"Actress," Alison said, correcting me.

"The actress," I repeated. "You know . . . she's on *Canyon Crossing*."

Maizie jumped off the bed and began nipping at my feet.

"Quit that," I told her.

"I warned you," Alison said.

"I've never seen *Canyon Crossing*," Rachel said.

"Yes, you have . . ." I told her. "Last year we watched it at my house . . . more than once."

"I don't remember," Rachel said.

"It's been cancelled," Alison said. "Mom's doing a new series. It's called *Franny on Her Own*. It won't be on until February. They're shooting in New York now. That's why we moved east. Leon's the head writer. He gets to decide what happens to all the characters."

"That's so exciting!" I said. "What's it like having Gena Farrell for a mother?"

"She's the only mother I've ever known." Alison stacked the books on her desk.

"But she's so famous!" I said.

Maizie growled. I wondered if it was true that she tried to bite reporters who asked too many questions.

"It doesn't matter that she's famous," Alison said. "When she's home she's Mom. The other stuff is just her work. It has nothing to do with me."

"You sound so well adjusted," Rachel said. "Kids of stars aren't supposed to be well adjusted. They're supposed to be neurotic."

"I can't help it if I'm not. Now could we please change the subject?"

I looked at Rachel. All three of us were quiet

for a minute. Then I said, "When you were little and you lived in France did you eat frogs' legs?"

Alison laughed. "Even when we change the subject you're still asking questions!"

"Stephanie likes to know everything about her friends," Rachel said, linking her arm through mine. "It's a sign that she cares."

Left Wing

The window in the second floor girls' room at school looks down on the playing field. I discovered this on Monday at the end of lunch period when I happened to look out that window. The soccer team was at practice. And who should be playing but Jeremy Dragon! I ran down to the cafeteria to tell Rachel and Alison. Then the three of us raced back up to the girls' room.

"He plays left wing!" Alison said.

"What does that mean?" I asked.

"That's his position," Alison said. "Look . . . he's trying for a goal!"

We held our breath. But he missed.

Since then we don't waste a lot of time in the cafeteria. As soon as we finish eating we come

room and spend the rest of lunch
... out the window. Jeremy Dragon
... s. Rachel says that means he's ex-

... ced how?" I asked.

"Experienced sexually," Rachel said.

"Really?" I asked. "How do you know that?"

"I read it," Rachel said.

"How far do you think he's gone?" Alison asked.

"Far," Rachel said.

"All the way?" Alison asked.

"Possibly," Rachel said.

"Just because he has hair on his legs?" I asked.

"That and other things," Rachel said.

"Like what?"

"I think what Rachel means," Alison said to me, "is that his body is very mature."

"Well, so is Rachel's," I said. "She has breasts and she gets her period."

"Really?" Alison said to Rachel. "You get your period?"

"Yes," Rachel said. "I've had it since fifth grade."

"I haven't had mine yet," Alison said.

"Neither has Steph," Rachel said.

"And that's the whole point," I told her. "*Your* body is developed and you don't have any experience. You haven't even kissed a boy."

"Jeremy Dragon is in ninth grade," Rachel said. "I certainly expect to have kissed a boy by the time I'm in ninth grade."

"I've already kissed two boys," Alison said.

Rachel and I looked at her. "Real kisses?" I asked.

"Yes."

"When did this happen?" Rachel asked.

"Last year. I kissed one at the beach and the other in the courtyard at school."

"How old were these boys?" Rachel asked.

"My age. Sixth grade."

"Kissing a sixth grade boy isn't the same as kissing someone like Jeremy Dragon," Rachel said. "Kissing Jeremy Dragon would be a whole different story."

Alison looked out the window. After a minute she said, "I see what you mean."

Mr. Kravitz

Mr, Kravitz, the exterminator, came to our house in a white truck that had KRAVITZ—SINCE 1967 printed in small letters on the door. He wore a dark blue jumpsuit with *Ed* stitched on the pocket. He had a brown and white dog with him. A beagle, I think. He brought the dog into our house. "This is Henry," Mr. Kravitz said. "He's trained to find termites."

"We don't have termites," Mom told him. "We have mice."

Mr. Kravitz looked at his notebook. "Oh, that's right." He laughed and shook his head. "Well, Henry's not a bad mouser, for a dog."

Mr. Kravitz and Henry followed Mom into the kitchen. Then, as if she'd just remembered I was there, she said, "This is my daughter, Stephanie."

"How do, Stephanie," Mr. Kravitz said.

"Mr. Kravitz bought the yellow house," Mom reminded me.

"I know," I told her.

"And we're certainly enjoying it," Mr. Kravitz said.

"I'm glad," Mom said. "Well . . . I'll let you get down to business, Mr. Kravitz. I hope you can clear up our problem."

"I'll do my best," Mr. Kravitz said.

Mom went upstairs to work at her computer, which she's moved from the den to her bedroom. I went to the refrigerator to get a glass of juice. "Do you use traps?" I asked Mr. Kravitz.

"No."

"What do you use?"

"Something else."

"What?"

"Does it make a difference?"

"Yes."

"Why?"

"Because my brother and I don't believe in violence."

"I don't use anything violent."

"What do you use?"

Mr. Kravitz let out a deep breath. "I use something to discourage them from coming back."

"Poison?" I asked.

"We don't think of it that way."

"Oh," I said, drinking my apple juice. Then I remembered my manners. "Would you like a glass of juice?"

"No thank you," Mr. Kravitz said. His dog, Henry, was sniffing inside the cabinet under the sink.

"So, who sleeps in my old room?" I asked.

Mr. Kravitz was inside the cabinet now, poking around with a flashlight. "Which room would that be?" he said. His voice was muffled.

"Top of the stairs . . . first room to the left," I told him.

"Hmm . . . that would be my youngest son's room. He's in ninth grade at Fox Junior High."

"Really," I said, talking louder. "I go to Fox. I'm in seventh grade."

"Maybe you know Jeremy," Mr. Kravitz said.

"Jeremy?"

"Yes. Jeremy Kravitz. He's my son."

"I only know one Jeremy," I said. "And he's not your son. He wears a chartreuse jacket with a dragon on the back."

Mr. Kravitz backed out of the cabinet. "That's *my* jacket," he said, laughing.

"Your jacket?"

"Nineteen-sixty-two," Mr. Kravitz said, standing up. "I was a senior in high school then."

"Are you saying that the boy who wears that dragon jacket is your son?"

"That's right."

"And his name is Jeremy and he sleeps in my old room?"

"That's right."

"Excuse me," I said to Kravitz. "I've got to do my homework now." I had to call Alison and Rachel right away! I ran into the den to use the phone.

I called Rachel first. "You won't believe this," I began, "but . . ." I told her the whole story. "You've got to come right over."

"I'm practicing my flute now," Rachel said.

"Rachel . . ." I said, "we are talking about Jeremy Dragon whose father happens to be standing in my kitchen. . . ."

"All right. . . ." Rachel said. "I'll be over in a few minutes."

I didn't have to convince Alison. She ran all the way around the pond and arrived at my house breathless. When Rachel got here the three of us went into the kitchen and I introduced them to Mr. Kravitz.

"Are you really Jeremy's father?" Rachel asked in her most mature voice.

Mr. Kravitz was spreading a white powder inside our cabinets. "Has Jeremy been giving you trouble?" he asked, looking up at us. "Has Jeremy been rude to you?"

I love how parents always assume the worst about their kids. "No," I said. "We're just curious because he rides our bus."

"And we're interested in that jacket he wears," Rachel said. "It's a very unusual jacket."

I tried to catch her attention but I couldn't.

"Actually it could be a valuable antique," Rachel continued. "I know because my aunt, who lives in New Hampshire, is in the antique business."

"The jacket was his," I said to Rachel, nodding in Mr. Kravitz' direction.

"Oh," Rachel said. "I didn't mean to insult you, Mr. Kravitz. I only meant that some day that jacket could be considered an antique. I didn't mean it was that old right now."

"I'm not insulted," Mr. Kravitz said.

Henry continued to sniff around our kitchen.

"Does your dog talk?" I asked Mr. Kravitz.

"Henry communicates," Mr. Kravitz said, as if my question was perfectly normal, "but he doesn't speak."

"Only one in seventeen million dogs can talk in words," I told him.

"Is that right?" Mr. Kravitz asked.

I didn't tell him about Maizie. It wasn't my business. If Alison wanted him to know she could tell him.

"Now girls . . ." Mr. Kravitz finally said, "I'd really like to spend more time chatting with you but I've got work to do here."

"Well . . . it's been very nice meeting you, Mr. Kravitz," Rachel said.

"Same here," Alison said.

"Likewise," Mr. Kravitz said, from inside another cabinet.

The three of us went outside and ran down to the pond. "Can you believe Jeremy Dragon sleeps in my old room?"

"Too bad you didn't sell your house with the furniture," Rachel said. "Then he'd be sleeping in your bed!"

The idea of Jeremy Dragon sleeping in my bed made me feel funny all over.

"You're blushing, Steph!" Alison said.

"Your face is purple!" Rachel sang.

"Excuse me," I said, walking between them. "I think I need to cool off." I went down to the edge of the pond and waded into the water, scaring the ducks, who paddled out of my way.

Rachel yelled, "Steph . . . what are you doing?"

And Alison called, "Steph . . . come out!"

"It feels great!" I sang, splashing around. "Come on in . . ."

"Stephanie!" Rachel shouted, "it's not a swimming pond!"

"So . . . who's swimming?"

They couldn't believe I'd gone into the pond with all my clothes on. Neither could my mother, who happened to be in the kitchen when I came home. "Stephanie . . . what on earth?"

"I didn't mean to get wet," I told her. "It just happened."

Dad's Laugh

Dad called from Hawaii. "Are the waves huge?" I asked.

"I haven't had a chance to get to the beach."

"Dad . . . how can you be in Hawaii and not get to the beach?"

"I'm here to work, Steph."

"I know . . . but still . . ."

"I'll try to get to the beach tomorrow . . . okay?"

"Okay. And send us some of that peanut brittle . . . the kind with macadamia nuts."

"I don't think peanut brittle is good for your braces."

"Well, then . . . send shells from the beach . . . or sand."

"I'll try," Dad said. "So what's new at home?"

I told him about our first dead mouse. "Mom found him in the cabinet under the sink . . . she practically fainted . . . so I lifted him out by his tail . . . dropped him into a Baggie . . . and tossed him in the trash can."

Dad laughed. I love to make him laugh. When he does he opens his mouth wide and you can see his gold fillings. "Wait . . . I'm not finished," I said, "because after I tossed him in the trash I forgot to put the bunjie cords back on the can . . . so that night the raccoons got into it and made a mess! So guess who had to clean up . . . and guess who almost missed the school bus?"

Dad kept on laughing. I'm definitely best in my family at making him laugh. But we don't get to laugh that much over the phone.

"So how's the weather?" Dad finally asked.

"Nice," I told him. "It's getting to be fall."

13

Remarkable Eyes

Mrs. Remo wears contact lenses. She's always telling us about them. She got them before school started so she's worn them for two months now. This morning she was rubbing her eye. Then she said, "Oh no . . ." and motioned for us to be quiet. "I think I've lost a contact lens. I need someone to help me find it."

Hands shot up around the room.

Eric Macaulay called out, "I've got perfect vision, Mrs. Remo. I'll find it for you."

"All right, Eric," Mrs. Remo said.

Eric shoved his chair back so hard it crashed into my desk, knocking over my books, which I had stacked like a pyramid. He raced up to the front of the room.

"Be careful where you step, Eric," Mrs. Remo said. "The lens is very fragile. I hope it's fallen onto my desk, not the floor."

But Eric didn't even bother to look on Mrs. Remo's desk. He stood right up close to her and seemed to be examining her dress, which was a dark green knit, with short sleeves. He didn't touch her, but the way he stared must have made her uncomfortable because she laughed nervously and said, "What *are* you doing, Eric?"

"Trying to find your lens," Eric said, "so please don't move."

I would have been very embarrassed to have Eric Macaulay examine me that closely, especially across my chest.

But then, halfway between Mrs. Remo's left shoulder and her waist, Eric plucked something off her dress. "Aha!" he said. "Got it!" He held it up for Mrs. Remo to see.

"Why, Eric . . ." Mrs. Remo said, taking the lens off his finger, "you must have remarkable eyes! How did you know it would be on my dress?"

"My mother wears contacts," Eric said. "Whenever she thinks she's lost one it's always stuck to her clothes."

"Thank you, Eric," Mrs. Remo said.

The class applauded and Eric took a bow.

Alison leaned across the aisle and whispered, "He's so cute!"

I made a face. Eric is too impossible to be cute.

On his way back to his desk Eric stopped next to Alison's. "Do you wear contacts, Thumbelina?"

He's been calling her Thumbelina since the second week of school but she doesn't seem to mind.

"No," Alison told him. "My eyes are as perfect as yours."

"Too bad . . ." Eric said, "because I wouldn't mind finding your lost lenses."

Alison started to giggle and once she gets started she can't stop.

As soon as Mrs. Remo had her lens back in place she held up a flyer and said, "I've got an announcement, class. The seventh grade bake sale will be held a week from Monday. The first . . ." She stopped and shook her head. "All right, Alison . . . either calm down or share the joke with the rest of us."

Alison covered her mouth with both hands to keep from laughing out loud but I could tell she still had the giggles.

Mrs. Remo continued with her announcement. "The first $150 will be used to donate food baskets to the needy. Anything over that will go to the seventh grade activity fund. Last year's seventh grade class earned enough to hold a winter dance."

A winter dance, I thought. Now that sounds interesting.

"So . . ." Mrs. Remo went on, "we need to appoint a bake sale chairperson . . . someone to keep track of who's baking what."

"Mrs. Remo . . ." Eric called, waving his arm.

"Yes, Eric?"

"I nominate Peter Klaff as chairperson. He's very organized. When I run for President he's going to be my campaign manager."

Was Eric planning to run for President of Fox Junior High, I wondered, or President of the United States?

"Peter . . ." Mrs. Remo said, "would you like to be chairperson of the bake sale?"

Everyone looked at Peter Klaff. He's shorter than me and much thinner. He has pale blond hair and eyebrows and lashes to match. Also, his ears stick out. I think it must run in the family because his mother and sister have the same kind of ears. You could see the red creeping up Peter's neck to his face. And you could see him gulping hard, as if he couldn't get enough air to breathe. He's so shy! But he managed to answer Mrs. Remo's question. He said, "Yes."

"Fine," Mrs. Remo said, "then it's all settled."

As Alison and I walked through the hall on

our way to first period class she began to sing a song she'd made up about a boy with remarkable eyes. "Well?" she said, when she'd finished.

I pretended to stick my finger down my throat.

"That bad?"

"No . . ." I said. "Worse!"

She bumped hips with me and we both laughed. But the next time she sang her song I found myself humming along.

14

Debate

Rachel says she has more important things on her mind than baking. She's trying out for the school debating team. Only two seventh graders will make it. She has to prepare a five-minute speech and present it at assembly on the afternoon of the bake sale.

"What's the subject of your speech?" I asked.

"Should wearing a seat belt be law or should it be up to the individual to decide?"

"That's easy," I said. "It should be law."

"I have to be able to argue both sides of the issue," Rachel explained, "even if I disagree with it."

"That's stupid."

"No . . . that's what debating is all about."

A few days later I went to Rachel's house after school. I couldn't stay long because I had an appointment at the orthodontist at four-thirty. Alison couldn't come over at all because she's got a rash on her foot and Leon took her to see Dr. Klaff.

Rachel was a wreck over her speech. "Look at my notes," she said, holding up a stack of 3x5 cards. "I've been working every night till ten."

"Don't worry so much," I told her. "After all, it's just five minutes."

"Do you have any idea how long five minutes really is?"

"Five minutes is five minutes," I said.

"I mean," she said, "do you know how it feels?"

"How it feels?" I asked.

"Yes," she said. "Look, I'll show you. Stand right there . . . right where you are . . ."

I was standing in the middle of her bedroom.

"Don't move," Rachel said.

"Okay."

"Now . . . tell me when you think five minutes is up. And don't look at your watch," she said. "Ready, set, go . . ."

I stood very still. I didn't move, except to scratch my leg. Burt and Harry were asleep on Rachel's bed. Rachel sat at her desk, shuffling her note cards. I wondered how Alison was doing at Dr. Klaff's. Alison says Peter Klaff likes me. She says he's always looking at me and that's how you can tell. But I'm not sure she's right. When Peter asked what I was bringing to the bake sale I told him I was partners with Alison and that we were baking brownies from an old family recipe. He didn't seem impressed.

I looked over at Rachel again. She was still at her desk, making more note cards. "Okay," I said. "Five minutes is up."

Rachel checked her watch. "Ha! It's only been one minute, twenty-four seconds."

"I can't believe it!"

"I told you five minutes feels like a long time!"

Mom made me puree of carrot and a baked potato for dinner that night, because after my braces are tightened I can't eat anything but soft, mushy foods. "Rachel's trying out for the debating team," I said, as I mashed my potato with butter. "She's got to make a five minute speech about seat belts."

"I'm sure she'll do fine," Mom said.

"I'm sure, too, but Rachel's worried. She wants to be the best."

"She's such a perfectionist," Mom said.

"I wouldn't mind being perfect," Bruce said.

"You mean you're not?" I asked.

"Very funny," he said.

"Be glad you're not," Mom said. "It's a hard way to go through life."

I tasted the carrot puree. Even though it looked like baby food it was delicious. Bruce watched me eat it. "I hope I never need braces," he said.

"It's temporary," I told him. "Some day I'll have a beautiful smile."

"Yeah . . . but what about the rest of your face?"

"Bruce!" Mom said.

"It's just a joke, Mom," he told her.

"He really wishes he looked like me," I said.

Bruce chuckled to himself.

We had vanilla pudding for dessert. "I'm thinking of trying out for symphonic band," I announced, as the pudding slid around in my mouth.

"Since when do you play an instrument?" Bruce asked.

"I'm trying out for percussion."

"Since when do you play drums?" Bruce asked.

"Ms. Lopez says I can learn . . . as long as I have a good sense of rhythm." I finished my pudding. "Do you think I have a good sense of rhythm?" I asked Mom.

"When you were little I'd give you a pot and a wooden spoon and you were happy for hours. If that's an indication I'd say yes."

"A pot and a wooden spoon," Bruce repeated, shaking his head and chuckling again.

The next time Dad called I asked him if he thought I had a good sense of rhythm.

He said, "You used to have a great time with a pot and a wooden spoon."

"That's exactly what Mom said."

"I guess we remember the same things."

I told him about the seventh grade bake sale and that Alison and I are going to bake Sadie Wishnik's brownies.

"Who's Sadie Wishnik?" Dad asked.

"Leon's mother."

"Who's Leon?"

"Alison's stepfather. And you know who Alison is," I told him, "she's my new friend."

"So Sadie Wishnik is her stepgrandmother?" Dad asked.

"I guess so," I said. "Anyway, we're going to Sadie's house to bake, on Sunday. She lives in New Jersey, near the ocean. And speaking of oceans . . . thanks for the box of shells from Hawaii. I've never seen such pretty ones. Did you find them yourself?"

Dad hesitated. "The truth?"

"Yes."

"I never did get to the beach. I bought them at a gift shop."

I knew it! I could tell by the way they were wrapped. But I didn't want Dad to feel bad so I said, "Maybe next time you'll get to the beach."

"Maybe so."

"Anyway . . . I love the shells!"

"I'm glad," Dad said. "So . . . what else is new at school?"

Dad is always asking what's new at school. I tell him what I think he wants to hear. What I don't tell him about is boys. I don't think he'd understand. If I told him that Peter Klaff stares at me he'd probably say, *Doesn't he know it's bad manners to stare?* And I certainly don't tell him about watching Jeremy Dragon at soccer. Dad would never understand that.

"What about your grades?" Dad asked.

"We haven't gotten any yet."

If Mom and Dad were in a debate and the subject was grades, Mom would say that what you actually learn is more important than the grades you get. Dad would argue that grades are an indication of what you've learned and how you handle responsibility. If I had to choose sides I'd choose Mom's.

15

Sadie Wishnik's Brownies

The rash on Alison's foot is called contact dermatitis. That means Alison's foot came into contact with something that caused the rash. What I don't get is, how can one foot come into contact with something the other foot doesn't? Dr. Klaff gave her a cream and told her to wear white cotton socks until the rash was gone.

Sunday morning, when I got to Alison's, she was waiting on her front steps. She had invited Rachel to come to Sadie Wishnik's, too. But Rachel said she had to stay home to work on her speech. I think the real reason Rachel wouldn't come is she gets carsick.

Gena Farrell came out of the house carrying

Maizie and a straw bag. She was wearing mirrored sunglasses. Her hair was tied back and she didn't have on any makeup. You couldn't tell she was famous. Leon followed, locking the door behind him. He carried the Sunday newspaper tucked under his arm.

As soon as we got going Gena pulled a needlepoint canvas out of her bag and began to stitch it.

"That's pretty," I said, trying to get a better look from the back seat. "What's it going to be?"

Gena took off her mirrored glasses, turned around, and faced me. She has big eyes—deep blue, like the color of the sky on a beautiful spring day. She held the needlepoint out, studied it for a minute and said, "A pillow, I think."

"Mom gave away twenty pillows last Christmas," Alison said.

Gena laughed. "I spend a lot of time sitting around and waiting on the set," she said. "So I do a lot of needlepointing. It relaxes me."

I couldn't believe Gena Farrell was talking to me as if we were both just regular people.

It took two and a half hours to get to Sadie's. Alison and I played Spit the whole time. Sadie lives in a place called Deal, in a big, old white house with a wraparound porch. She belongs to a group that brings food to people who are too old or sick to cook for themselves. It's called Meals on Wheels. When Leon told me about her, he sounded very proud.

Hearing about Sadie made me think of my grandparents. Gran Lola, who gave me my bee-sting locket, isn't the cooking kind of grandmother. She's a stockbroker in New York. She wears suits and carries handbags that match her shoes. I once counted the handbags in her closet. She had twenty-seven of them. Mom says that's because Gran Lola never throws anything away. Papa Jack is a stockbroker, too. He has an ulcer.

My father's parents are both dead. They died a week apart. I hate to think of Mom and Dad getting old and dying. It scares me. So I put it out of my mind.

Sadie was waiting for us on her porch. When she saw the car pull into the driveway she came down the stairs to greet us. She was very small, with white hair and dark eyes, like Leon's. She was wearing a pink sweat suit. She hugged Alison first. "My favorite granddaughter," she said, kissing both her cheeks.

"Your only granddaughter," Alison said. Then she introduced me. "This is Stephanie, my best friend in Connecticut."

I smiled, surprised by Alison's introduction.

Sadie shook my hand. "Any friend of Alison's is a friend of mine."

You could smell the ocean from Sadie's front porch. I took a few deep breaths. Sadie must have noticed because she said, "It's just three blocks away. You'll see for yourself this afternoon."

Inside, the table was set for lunch. As soon as Leon walked Maizie we sat down to eat. Everything tasted great. There's something about salt air that makes me really hungry.

After lunch Alison and I helped Sadie do the dishes. Then Sadie pushed up her sleeves and said, "Okay . . . now it's time to get down to business."

I love to bake. I especially love to separate eggs. Aunt Denise taught me how to do it without breaking the yolks, but for brownies you don't need to separate eggs.

"Grandma," Alison said, after we'd measured, mixed and divided the batter into six large baking pans, "don't you think we should write down the recipe for next time?"

"It's better to keep it up here," Sadie said, tapping her head. "That way, if you find yourself in Tahiti and you want to bake brownies, you won't have to worry."

We slid the pans into the ovens. "So . . ." Sadie said, "you'll have one hundred twenty full sized brownies or, if you cut them in half . . ."

"Two hundred forty," I said.

"I don't think we should cut them in half," Alison said, "because we want to sell each one for fifty cents. And that way we'll make . . . uh . . ."

"Sixty dollars," I said.

Sadie looked at me. "A mathematician!" she said. "A regular Einstein!"

"Not really," I told her, feeling my face flush. "Rachel's the mathematician. She couldn't come today because she gets car—" I caught myself just in time. "She couldn't come because she had to work on her speech."

"If we earn enough at this bake sale," Alison told Sadie, "the seventh grade will be able to have a winter dance."

"A dance!" Sadie said. "I used to love to go dancing. Nobody could hold a candle to my rumba. I could wiggle with the best of them. And you should see my mambo and samba and cha cha . . ." She began to sing and dance around the kitchen. "Come on . . ." she said, holding her hands out to us. "I'll teach you."

"I don't think we'll be doing the rumba at the seventh grade dance," Alison said.

"You never know," Sadie told her. "This way you'll be prepared."

First, Sadie taught us the basic box step. *Forward, to the side, together . . . backward, to the side, together.* Once we had that she taught us the rumba. She was about to teach us the samba when the timer on the oven went off. Sadie stuck a toothpick into the center of each pan to make sure the brownies were done. Then we set them on racks on the counter to cool.

"Now . . ." Sadie said, "if you'll excuse me, it's time for my siesta."

"Your siesta?" *I* said.

"Grandma never says nap," Alison explained. "Naps are for babies . . . right, Grandma?"

"Right."

While Sadie was taking her siesta Alison and I went to the beach with Leon and Gena. Leon held Maizie on a leash until we got there. Then he turned her loose and she took off, running first in one direction, then the other.

Leon and Gena sat on a jetty to watch the waves. Alison and I took off our shoes and socks. "What about your rash?" I asked. "I thought you have to wear a sock on that foot."

"I'm sure the salt water is good for it," Alison said.

It was windy on the beach, but sunny and warm for October. We rolled up our jeans and ran along the water's edge, laughing. Alison's long, black hair whipped across her face, making me wish mine would hurry and grow. Maizie ran alongside us, looking up, as if to say, *How much longer are we going to play this game?*

I was having the best time. I like being with Alison. I like being her friend.

Maizie barked.

"Are you having fun, too?" I asked her.

She barked again.

"What's she saying?" I called to Alison, who was ahead of me.

"Nothing," Alison called back. "She's a dog."

"What do you mean?" I asked, catching up with her.

Alison flopped down. Maizie rolled over and over in the sand. "Do you really believe that dogs can talk?" Alison asked.

"Only one in seventeen million," I said, sitting beside her.

Alison laughed and lay back. Maizie jumped on her.

"You mean she *can't* talk?"

Alison shielded her eyes from the sun and looked at me. "You didn't really believe me, did you?"

"Of course not," I said, drawing a face in the sand with my finger. "I was just playing along with you."

Alison sat up. Sand fell from her hair. "You *did* believe me!"

"I suppose now you think I'm *gullible*," I said.

"I don't know what that means," Alison said.

"It means when a person is easily tricked . . . when a person believes anything. I know because I looked it up one time."

"I don't think you're like that," Alison said. "I think you're a lot like me." She wrestled with Maizie for a minute. When Maizie escaped she said, "I only told you she could talk because I wanted you to like me. I wanted us to be friends."

"We are friends," I said.

"Best friends?"

I picked up a handful of sand. "Rachel and I have been best friends since second grade," I said, letting the sand trickle through my fingers.

"You mean you've never had more than one best friend at a time?" Alison asked.

"No . . . have you?"

"Sure . . . almost every year."

I looked at her. "So you're saying the three of us can be best friends?"

"Sure," Alison said.

"Great!"

"But don't tell Rachel about Maizie, okay? I'll tell her myself . . . when the time is right."

"Okay." I looked down the beach at the jetty. Leon and Gena were kissing.

16

La Crème De La Crème

Sadie's brownies were a big hit. Kids kept asking, "Who baked these? They're great!" We saved one for Rachel. She was too worried about her speech to get to the bake sale.

Jeremy Dragon came back for a second brownie, then a third. Alison handed him the brownies and I took his money. That way we each got to touch him three times. It's good the brownies were individually wrapped because his hands were dirty.

Even Mrs. Remo bought one and when she tasted it she said, "These are incredible . . . they're so moist. Do you have the recipe?"

"It's in my grandmother's head," Alison told her.

"See if you can get her to write it down," Mrs. Remo said, licking her lips. "These are definitely *la crème de la crème.*"

Alison smiled. Ever since Mrs. Remo mispronounced her name on the first day of school she's been trying French phrases on her.

"What's *la crème de la crème* mean?" I asked Alison when Mrs. Remo was gone.

"It means *the best of the best.*"

At the end of the day we had the debate assembly. Five kids from seventh grade were trying out. The only one I knew, besides Rachel, was this boy, Toad. His name is really Todd but everyone calls him Toad, including his family. He went to my elementary school but he wasn't in my sixth grade class.

Toad spoke first, then two girls I didn't know, then a boy who's in my social studies class, then Rachel. She had brushed her hair away from her face, making her look younger than usual, and prettier. I know her so well I never think about her looks. I forget about the way her lower lip twitches when she's scared.

That morning, when I'd called for Rachel, her mother had been giving her a last minute lecture about the debate. "Wear your height as if you're proud of it . . . shoulders back, head high."

"Yeah . . . yeah . . ." Rachel had said. She'd heard it all before.

Mrs. Robinson had planted a kiss on Rachel's cheek. "I know you'll be the best. You always are."

Now, as Rachel walked across the stage, my heart started to beat very fast. I could tell she was trying to take her mother's advice but somehow she wound up walking as if she were in pain.

When she got to the lectern she tapped the microphone to make sure it was still working, then cleared her throat twice. Her voice trembled as she began to speak but once she got going her body relaxed and her voice changed into that grownup one she uses when she wants to get attention. A hush fell over the audience. You could tell everyone was listening to what she had to say. She was definitely *la crème de la crème* of debaters.

When she finished the audience applauded the same way they had for the others. Then Mr. Diamond, my English teacher, stepped up to the microphone to make some announcements. The first was that we had made $316 at the bake sale that morning. Everyone cheered, especially Alison and me because Sadie's brownies had brought in close to a fifth of the total! Next, Mr. Diamond told us we'd be able to donate food baskets to the needy on both Thanksgiving *and* Christmas. Everybody cheered again. And then he said we'd earned enough to have a winter dance on Ground Hog Day, February 2. The cheering grew louder.

"That's my birthday," I whispered to Alison, who was sitting next to me.

"You're so lucky!" she said.

Another teacher handed Mr. Diamond a slip of paper. "Okay . . ." he said, "here are the results of this afternoon's competition. The two newest members of the debating team are . . ." He hesitated for a minute, making my stomach turn over, "Todd Scrudato and Rachel Robinson."

Toad and Rachel came forward to shake Mr. Diamond's hand. Rachel was smiling and she walked more like herself. I felt myself choke up. I reached over and squeezed Alison's hand. She squeezed mine back.

The Alison Monceau Story

I have never understood what makes some kids so popular. I've been trying to figure it out for years. Almost from the first week of school you could tell Alison was going to be the most popular girl in our homeroom and it's not because her mother is Gena Farrell. Nobody knows about that but Rachel and me and we are sworn to secrecy. The funny thing is, Alison doesn't even try to be popular. It's just that everyone wants to be her friend. I've made a list with reasons why.

1. She is very friendly.
2. She never has anything bad to say about anyone.

3. She doesn't have bad moods.
4. She laughs a lot.
5. She is funny.
6. She has nice hair.
7. She looks different than the rest of us because she is Vietnamese. Looking different can either work for you or against you. In Alison's case it works for her.

Alison knows how to be popular without being snobby, which is more than I can say for Amber Ackbourne. She's the leader of the snobbiest group of girls in seventh grade. And now she wants to be Alison's friend. She's always coming up to her in homeroom. But Alison can see right through her.

The boys like Alison, too. They just have different ways of showing it. They like to tease her, the way Eric Macaulay does, calling her Thumbelina and shooting rubber bands in her direction. Rachel says it's demeaning to be called Thumbelina. She says Alison should put a stop to it right now, before it gets out of hand.

"He only calls me that because I'm small," Alison said the other day at my house. "You know that fairy tale about the girl who's smaller than a thumb . . . there's even a song about her." Alison began to sing and dance around my room. She's a very good dancer. She must take after

Sadie Wishnik. When she finished she fell back on my bed, laughing. I laughed too. Finally, so did Rachel. Alison has a way of making people feel good.

Soon all three of us were singing the Thumbelina song and by the time Rachel went home she said, "Well . . . maybe it's not so demeaning."

Alison also knows how to flirt. I've been watching to see how she does it. She kind of teases the boys and giggles. You can learn a lot by watching a popular person in action. You can learn how to act and how not to act. Mom is always telling me to be myself but there are times when I don't know what being myself means. Sometimes I feel grown up and other times I feel like a little kid. I seem to be more than one person.

That's exactly how I felt last Wednesday. It was raining really hard. Alison came to my house after school. Rachel couldn't come because she had a music lesson. We were sitting in the kitchen, eating doughnuts and playing Spit, when we got to talking about the games we used to play when we were little. It turned out we'd both collected Barbies. So I got the idea to go down to the basement and dig out my old Barbie dolls, which I haven't seen since fourth grade. I found them in a carton marked *Steph's Old Toys*. I carried the Barbie case up to my room, closed the door and Alison and I played all afternoon, dressing and undressing my three Barbies, while we made up silly stories for them to act out.

One of the stories was *Barbie Is Adopted*. After we'd finished, I asked Alison how it feels to be adopted for real.

"How would I know?" she asked. "I was adopted when I was four months old. I don't know what it feels like not to be adopted."

"But do you ever think about your biological mother?" I asked. I had seen this movie on TV about an adopted girl and when she was eighteen she decided to search for her biological mother.

"Sometimes I think about her," Alison said, "about how young and poor she was. She was just fifteen when she had me. But I'm happy with Gena and Leon. If I had to choose parents I'd choose them."

"I'd choose mine, too," I said, "except I'd make sure my father got a job where he didn't have to travel."

"What does he do anyway?"

"He's in public relations."

"When's he coming home?" Alison asked.

"Not until Thanksgiving."

"You must really miss him."

"Yeah . . . I do."

Later, when we packed up my Barbies and put them away, we vowed never to tell anyone we had played with them that afternoon.

The next day I was sitting in French class day-dreaming about Alison. About how her life sounds just like a fairy tale. It would make a good movie, I thought. It would be called *The Alison Monceau Story*. It would star Gena Farrell as Alison's mother and Alison as herself and I would play her best friend. *Stephanie Behrens Hirsch* it would say on the screen. Maybe Rachel could play Alison's biological mother. With makeup and a wig she could probably look Vietnamese and she could certainly look fifteen. Jeremy Dragon could play . . .

"Stephanie!" Mrs. Hillerman shouted. "Will you please wake up!"

"What . . . me?"

The class laughed.

"I've lost my place," I said.

"I don't think you ever had it," Mrs. Hillerman said. And then she said something to me in French, something I didn't understand, and the whole class laughed again.

18

Macbeth

> *Double, double, toil and trouble;*
> *Fire burn and cauldron bubble.*

Rachel taught us this poem from *Macbeth*, by William Shakespeare. We're going to dress up as the three witches from the play and recite the poem instead of saying "Trick or Treat" on Halloween. We're not interested in "Trick or treating." We're interested in using it as an excuse to get into a certain person's yellow house.

On Halloween night we put on the weirdest clothes we could find, plus junk jewelry and witches' hats. We also used gobs of makeup from Gena Farrell's makeup collection. Alison showed us how to do our eyes. When Gena saw us she said, "The three of you are really something!"

It took us twenty minutes to walk to my old house. Once you're on Pine Tree Road you still have to go down a quiet lane to the end, then up a long, steep driveway, through the woods.

"How long did you live here?" Alison asked.

"Almost all my life until last summer."

The outside lights were on and a carved pumpkin sat on each side of the front door. "It's a big house," Alison said, looking around.

"Yeah. . . ." I nodded and rang the bell. It was hard to think of another family living in my house.

Jeremy answered the door. He wasn't wearing his chartreuse jacket. "Witches," he said, looking us over.

We stepped into the foyer. "Not just any witches," Alison told him. "We're the three from *Macbeth*."

"*Macbeth* . . ." Jeremy said. "Wasn't that on TV?"

"*Macbeth* is a play by William Shakespeare," I told him, as if I knew all about it.

"Oh, *that Macbeth*." Jeremy said.

Rachel, who hadn't spoken yet, gave us the sign to recite our poem.

> "Double, double, toil and trouble;
> Fire burn and cauldron bubble."

"Yeah, I know what you mean," Jeremy said, when we'd finished. Henry, the termite dog, came down the stairs and sniffed us. Then he wandered off through the dining room.

"I used to live here," I told Jeremy, as he dropped a Heath bar into each of our bags.

"Oh, yeah . . ." he said, "my father mentioned something about a girl who used to live here."

"Stephanie," I said. "Stephanie Hirsch. We met at my mother's travel agency . . . remember?"

He gave me a blank look.

"You and your friends needed brochures for a school project," I reminded him.

"Oh, right . . ." he said. "You look different."

"I wasn't wearing a witch's hat that day."

"And you bought brownies from us at the bake sale," Alison said.

"Those brownies were the best," Jeremy said. "I could've put away a dozen." Then he looked right at Rachel and he said, "You're Rachel, right?"

Rachel didn't say anything. She just gave us the sign to recite our poem again.

> "Double, double, toil and trouble;
> Fire burn and cauldron bubble."

When we were outside I grabbed Rachel's arm and said, "He knew your name."

Rachel ignored me. So I asked, "How does he know your name?"

"How should I know?" Rachel said, sounding angry, as if it were my fault Jeremy knew her name. She ran the rest of the way down the driveway and when we were back on the road she said, "We're too old for this! I don't know what got into me! I don't know why I agreed to it!" She sounded on the verge of tears. "I'm going home!"

"Don't go now," Alison said, running to catch up with her. "We haven't been anywhere yet. We haven't been to Eric Macaulay's or Peter Klaff's or . . ."

"You're going to spoil all our fun!" I called, chasing Rachel, who was walking very fast. "How can we be the three witches from *Macbeth* without you?"

Rachel sniffled. "Okay . . . but I'm never doing this again."

"Fine," I told her. "You don't have to."

But we didn't have much fun after that. So we headed for home.

The next day, at the end of math class, Mr. Burns gave me a note to take to another math teacher, Mrs. Godfrey. I got to Mrs. Godfrey's room just as the bell rang and the door opened. Jeremy Dragon was the first one out. "Hey, Macbeth . . ." he said when he saw me.

At least he recognized me this time.

Then Dana Carpenter came out. "Hi, Steph . . . what are you doing here?"

"I've got a note for Mrs. Godfrey," I said. "What class is this?"

"Enriched math."

"Oh," I said.

"I've got to run," Dana said. "See you later."

"Okay."

I waited while the ninth graders trudged out of Mrs. Godfrey's room. Then, just as I was about to go in with the note, who should come out but Rachel!

We stared at each other.

"What are you doing here?" Rachel asked, sharply.

"I've got a note for Mrs. Godfrey," I said. "What are *you* doing here?"

Rachel brushed past me and began to walk down the hall. I followed her. "I *said* what are *you* doing here?"

"They switched me to this class."

"They switched you to this class . . . to *enriched* math?"

"Yes."

"And you never told me?" I said. "You never said anything about it?"

"What should I have said?" Rachel stopped and we faced each other.

"You should have said that you were switched to *enriched* ninth grade math!" I told her. "That's what you *should* have said."

"Will you stop saying it like that!" Rachel's lower lip quivered.

"Like what?"

"Like it's something bad I've done."

"I didn't say it was bad," I told her. "I just said it's a big surprise!"

Rachel didn't say anything.

"So how long have you been in this enriched ninth grade class?" I asked.

"Since the second week of school," Rachel said, quietly, looking at the floor.

"The second week of school!" I said, my voice growing louder. "Well, isn't that interesting! Were you ever going to tell me?"

"I wanted to," Rachel said, "but I was afraid you'd be mad."

"Mad!" I said. "Why should I be mad? Just because Jeremy Dragon knows your name and you tell me you don't know how? *I* should be mad over a little thing like that? Just because I'm supposed to be your best friend and you keep a secret like this from me?"

"I wasn't sure I would like the class," Rachel said. "I didn't think there was any point in telling you until I'd made up my mind. And I didn't know, until last night, that he knew my name."

I felt this huge bubble of anger rising from my stomach. When it got to my throat I shouted, "Oh . . . who cares!" and I marched away from Rachel, holding my books tight against my chest.

"Look," Rachel said, keeping up with me, "I didn't ask to be born this way."

"What way?" I snapped.

"The way I am."

"What way is that?"

"Smart." Rachel practically spit out the word.

"You're not just smart," I told her.

"Okay . . . so I'm not just smart. It still isn't my fault. It just happened. It's not something I work at, you know. It's not something I especially like about myself. Most of the time I wish I could be like everyone else . . . like you!"

"Thanks a lot!"

"I meant that in a friendly way, Steph."

I didn't respond. I didn't know what to say. I didn't even know what I was feeling. All I knew was this was the first time Rachel had ever kept a secret from me.

"Does this mean you don't want to be my friend anymore?" Rachel's voice broke, as if she might cry any second.

"No," I said. "It doesn't mean anything except you should have told me about that math class yourself."

"You're right," Rachel said, "I know that now."

The second bell rang. I ran to my next class and didn't realize, until I got there, that I still hadn't given Mrs. Godfrey the note from Mr. Burns. So I ran all the way back to Mrs. Godfrey's class and was late getting to my own.

19

Confessions

I know, deep down, it's not Rachel's fault she's
so smart or that she was switched to enriched
math. But that doesn't mean I have to like it.
How can you be best friends with someone who
keeps secrets from you? Important secrets, like
being in enriched math.

I didn't say anything to Alison about Rachel
that afternoon. I didn't say anything because I
didn't have the chance. Leon picked us up after
school and drove us to town. It was raining. The
three of us had to go to the library to look up
information for our first social studies report.
All the seventh graders have the same assignment: to do a report on someone who has made
a major difference to the world.

Leon dropped us off at TCBY, the frozen yogurt place. The letters stand for The Country's Best Yogurt. Alison is really into frozen yogurt. She says everybody in California loves it. Rachel likes it, too. I used to think it was gross but now I'm getting used to it. I ordered a hot fudge sundae which the menu describes as swirls of french vanilla yogurt with hot fudge and whipped topping sprinkled with pecans. Alison and Rachel ordered Smoothies. A Smoothie is a yogurt and fruit juice drink.

When our order was ready we carried it to a table. As soon as we sat down Rachel said to Alison, "I have something to tell you." She took a long sip of her Smoothie. "Remember those math tests we took the first week of school?"

"Uh huh," Alison said. "That's how Mr. Burns found out I'd lost my skills."

Mr. Burns is always telling Alison she's lost her skills. Alison keeps trying to explain she never had those skills in the first place.

"Well . . ." Rachel said, glancing at me, then turning her attention back to Alison. "After those tests I got transferred to another math class." She paused and took another sip of her Smoothie. "I got transferred to a more advanced math class."

"I'm not surprised," Alison said.

"It's enriched ninth grade math," Rachel said.

"No kidding," Alison said. She licked some Smoothie off her upper lip.

"I'm in Dana Carpenter's class," Rachel said.

"I like Dana," Alison said.

"And Jeremy Dragon is in my class, too."

Alison put down her glass and did look really surprised. Now she's going to let Rachel have it, I thought. Now she's going to tell her that friends don't keep secrets like that.

But all Alison said was, "I never knew Jeremy was smart. I mean, he thought *Macbeth* was a TV show!"

"I guess he's smarter at some things than others," Rachel said.

"So is that what you wanted to tell me?" Alison asked, slurping up the rest of her Smoothie.

"Yes," Rachel said.

"Well, congratulations," Alison said. "Maybe you could help me with my decimals and percentages. I can't do pre-algebra until I've got them down."

"Sure," Rachel said, "any time."

I could see the relief on Rachel's face, and to tell the truth I couldn't understand why Alison reacted to Rachel's news as if it was just ordinary school stuff. But I didn't say anything. I just sat there spooning up my yogurt sundae, wishing it were ice cream instead.

"I have something to tell you, too," Alison said to Rachel. "Maizie doesn't talk. I made that up to get you and Steph to like me."

"I've always known that." Rachel looked at me. "It's Steph who believes everything she hears."

"She already knows about Maizie," Alison said.

"Really?" Rachel said. "Since when?"

"Since the day we went to Sadie Wishnik's house to bake brownies," Alison told her.

"That was weeks ago," Rachel said, glaring at me. I spooned up the sauce from the bottom of my dish and licked it off the spoon.

"I asked Steph to let me tell you myself," Alison explained.

"I see," Rachel said, quietly.

"Just like you got to tell Alison about your enriched math class yourself," I said to Rachel.

"You knew about her math class?" Alison asked me.

"I wouldn't exactly say I knew . . . I just found out today . . . by accident."

We just sat there. No one said anything. Finally Rachel stood up and gathered her books. "We should get going. We've got a lot to do at the library."

Alison and I got our things together, too. Outside, it had stopped raining.

"Who are you doing your report on?" Rachel asked Alison as we headed for the library.

"Martha Graham," Alison said. "She practically invented modern dance. What about you?" she asked Rachel.

"Margaret Mead. She was a famous anthropologist. How about you, Steph . . . who are you doing?"

"Jane Fonda."

"Jane Fonda!" Rachel said. "What major difference has she made to the world?"

"She got a lot of people to exercise," I said.

Rachel snorted. "I don't think that's the kind of difference our teachers have in mind."

"I'm not so sure," Alison said. "Jane Fonda is a very important person. Everybody in L.A. . . ."

"We're talking about the world," Rachel said, "not L.A."

"I know," Alison said, "but besides exercise she's a very good actress. My mother's always saying she'd love to be offered half the roles Jane Fonda gets."

Rachel shook her head. "I don't know about the two of you."

That night I went to Mom's room. She was stretched out on her chaise lounge, reading.

That's her favorite place to relax. "Rachel's been transferred to enriched math and she never even told me."

Mom looked at me over the top of her glasses. They're half glasses. She wears them for reading. She tucks in her chin when she looks over them, giving her face a funny expression.

"She's so smart!" I said, sitting on the edge of the chaise lounge.

"You're smart, too, honey," Mom said.

"Not smart like Rachel." I picked up a small, white pillow and held it to me.

"Rachel is gifted," Mom said.

"Gifted," I repeated, trying out the word.

"Does it bother you that she's been placed in enriched math?"

"It's not just any enriched math," I said. "It's ninth grade enriched math."

"You know, Steph . . . life isn't easy for Rachel."

"Are you kidding? She can get straight A's without even trying."

"I'm not talking about grades," Mom said.

I didn't say anything.

"You're not going to let this math class come between you, are you?"

I played with the lace ruffle on the pillow. "I guess not . . . unless Rachel does." I didn't want to think about Rachel anymore. So I looked across the room at the group of family photos on the wall. There's one I especially like of Mom and Dad. He's carrying her piggy-back and she's laughing so hard her eyes are closed. "I can't wait until Thanksgiving," I said. "I can't wait to see Dad!"

I told Dad I was counting the days when he called the next night.

"So am I," Dad said. "What's new in school?"

"I made symphonic band . . . percussion."

"Congratulations!"

"And in math we're following the stock market."

"That sounds interesting."

"It is. We each get to pick three stocks and pretend they're ours. I picked Reebok, Revlon and Jiffy Lube."

"That's quite an assortment."

"I know."

"How's the weather?"

"It's been raining," I said. "But today the sun came out again." I paused, trying to come up with something else that would interest Dad. "Have you heard about Bruce?" I asked.

"What about him?"

"Well . . ." I began, but Bruce grabbed the phone out of my hand and said, "I'll tell him myself."

Bruce has entered a national contest. *Kids for Peace* it's called. He's made a poster and sent it to Boston, where it will be judged. The three winners will get a free trip to Washington where they'll meet the President. In some ways I hope Bruce does win the contest. In other ways I hope he doesn't. I don't know how I'd feel having a famous brother. Probably everyone would compare me to him and ask, *What contests have you won, Stephanie?* And I'd have to think of some clever answer like, *I don't believe in contests. Contests don't prove anything.*

I wonder if Jessica and Charles feel that way, having a younger sister like Rachel. I wonder if they're always trying to prove that they're as good as she is. Lucky for me Bruce isn't gifted. He's just a regular kid who happens to have made a great poster.

20

Things

Mom and Aunt Denise are trying to decide whether to make a vegetable stuffing or a chestnut stuffing for the Thanksgiving turkey. They don't actually put the stuffing inside the turkey. They make it as a side dish. Mom says it's healthier to roast the turkey without stuffing it. I don't see why they call it stuffing when it isn't.

We're going to have fourteen to dinner. Everyone is family except for Carla, Mom's best friend from college, and her little girl, Katie, who is eight. Carla is a widow. Her husband was killed while he was crossing the street. Some guy in a van plowed into him. The guy didn't even have a driver's license. Katie was only a baby at the time. She never got to know her father. Mom says some people have more than their fair share of trouble. But Carla has a very good job. She produces a news show for NBC.

I asked Mom if I could make place cards this year because everyone always stands around at Thanksgiving waiting to be told where to sit. And while they're waiting the food gets cold. Mom said place cards sounded like a good idea. I made them out of purple colored paper. I drew a flower on each one and tried to keep my letters from going uphill when I printed the names.

Then I made a seating chart, like the one Mrs. Remo used the first week of school, before she'd memorized our names. I put myself between Dad and Katie. I put Bruce next to cousin Howard. I would never sit next to Howard. He's seventeen and disgusting. He burps after every mouthful. Then he tells us that in some countries burping is considered a great compliment to the cook. If you don't burp, Howard says, you're a very rude guest. Howard also lets it out the other end. I asked him at our Passover seder, last spring, if that's also considered a compliment in some countries. He just laughed. I'm so glad I don't have a brother like him.

Mom says he's just going through a phase and that in a few years he'll be just like his brother, Stanley, who goes to college. I don't know if that's good or bad. Stanley is such a bore!

On Wednesday, the day before Thanksg[iving], I couldn't concentrate in school. I kept think[ing] that in a few hours I would see Dad again. I pictured him in my mind. He's tall and thin, with a bony face. His eyes are grayish-blue and he wears aviator glasses. He's got a dimple in his chin, like Bruce. When he's very tired his shoulders slump. He'll probably be very tan from all that California sunshine, I thought. And he'll have presents for all of us—sweatshirts for Bruce and me, saying something about California, and for Mom, perfume and a lacy nightgown.

I was glad we had only half a day of school. During the last hour we had an all-school Thanksgiving assembly, which made the time go even faster. The chorus sang, the dancers danced and the symphonic band played. This was my debut as a percussionist. I got to play cymbals twice and chimes once. I made a mistake on chimes. But Ms. Lopez, the music teacher, gave me a reassuring look, as if my mistake hadn't mattered at all.

Aunt Denise picked me up after school. I always help her bake the pies for Thanksgiving dinner. She says she wishes she had a daughter like me. I don't blame her. Imagine someone as

g stuck with sons like

baking Aunt Denise and
tchen. "Has your mom been
he asked, as she handed me the
owl to dry.

"A t?" I asked.

"You ow," Aunt Denise said, "things . . ."

"Oh, *things*," I said. "Yeah . . . Mom bought me a book."

"A book?"

"Yeah . . . *Love and Sex in Plain Language*."

"Sex?"

"Yes, isn't that what you meant?"

Aunt Denise hesitated. "Sort of . . ."

"I'm home!" I called, when Aunt Denise dropped me off at five. I wanted to change before Dad got here. He's renting a car at Kennedy Airport and driving up to Connecticut.

"I'm upstairs. . . ." Mom called back. I went to her room. She had just stepped out of the shower and was wrapped in a big striped towel.

"What a day," she said, holding her head, "I have a headache *this* big . . ." She took a bottle of aspirin from her cabinet and gulped down two of them with water. "I've made reservations at Onion Alley for you and Bruce and Dad . . . at seven."

"What about you?" I asked.

"I'm going over to Denise's to help with the stuffing and the sweet potato pudding."

"But, Mom . . . this is Dad's first night home."

"I know, honey . . . but we've talked it over and he understands."

"But, Mom . . ." I began again. Then I remembered that they would be alone later. "Oh, I get it," I said, giving Mom a sly look.

"Really, Steph . . ." Mom said.

21

Dad

It was a nippy night and I shivered in my sweater as I waited outside for Dad. To keep warm I jumped in the leaves on our front lawn. I was glad it was already dark. I wouldn't want anyone to see me fooling around that way.

A car drove slowly down our street. I brushed myself off and watched, wondering if it could be Dad. It passed our house, stopped, then backed up, parking right in front. The door opened and Dad got out. I ran toward him. "Dad!" He hugged me and held me close. It felt so good to smell his special smell again, a combination of after-shave, butterscotch lifesavers and something else . . . something that's just him. He was wearing his same old brown suede jacket. It felt soft and familiar against my cheek.

When we were inside the house I noticed the bald spot on the back of his head had grown, or maybe it was just the way the wind had blown his hair. Also, he had no tan. I asked him about that right away.

He said, "I'm working long hours. I don't have time to sit in the sun."

He did look worn out. It's not good for him to be away from us, I thought. He probably has no one to cheer him up after a hard day at work.

"Didn't anybody ever tell you it's impolite to stare?" Dad said, laughing.

"What?"

"You were staring," he said again.

"I was?"

"Yes . . . so now it's my turn." He looked me over carefully. I don't know why but I suddenly felt shy. I guess it's because I'm a different person now, different than when Dad left. I hadn't even started seventh grade then. Now, I'm almost a teenager. Dad ruffled my hair.

"It's growing," I said, self-consciously, as I touched it. "It should be long again by spring."

"It looks fine the way it is," Dad said.

Bruce came racing down the stairs. Dad picked him up and swung him around. Then they kind of nuzzled and swatted each other's arms the way they do to show affection. "You look so big," Dad told Bruce.

"I haven't grown at all," Bruce said. "Not an inch."

"Well, you could have fooled me."

Mom came downstairs right behind Bruce. She and Dad hugged, but just for a minute. "How are you, Row?" Dad asked.

"I'm okay," Mom said.

You could tell they didn't want to get started in front of us.

I was right about the sweatshirts. Dad brought one for me that said *Los Angeles, City of Angels* and one for Bruce that said *Los Angeles Dodgers.* I don't know what he brought for Mom.

Dad had never even seen my new room so I grabbed him by the hand and led him upstairs.

"Look at all these posters," Dad said. "How come that one is on the ceiling?" He strained his neck to get a better view of Benjamin Moore.

"That one is special," I said. "You have to lie on the bed to really see him."

"Maybe later," Dad said.

He didn't seem surprised that just the three of us were going out to dinner. I guess he and Mom had worked out the details over the phone. We got to sit in a booth at Onion Alley. I ordered a calzone but I didn't eat much because Bruce and I talked non-stop through dinner. I told Dad all about Alison and how she used to live in Malibu, which she says isn't that far from Marina Del Rey, where Dad has his apartment. I told him about how she's lost her skills in math but that Rachel is going to help her get them back. I told him how well Alison and I get along and how much fun she is.

"It sounds as if you and Alison are best friends," Dad said, picking at his veal.

"I'm best friends with Rachel *and* Alison," I told him.

"Two best friends?" Dad asked.

"Two are better than one," I told him.

"Two best friends means she's never off the phone," Bruce said. "She just about lives in the pantry."

"The pantry?" Dad looked confused.

"That's where she hides with the phone," Bruce explained.

"If I had my *own* phone in my *own* room I wouldn't have to lock myself up in the pantry for privacy. At Crazy Eddie's you can get one for just $19.95. That's what I'd really like for my birthday."

"I don't think it's a question of how much a phone costs," Dad said. "I think it's more the idea of it."

"But you'll think about it, won't you?" I asked. "For my *thirteenth* birthday?"

"I'll discuss it with Mom."

I'll discuss it with Mom is Dad's version of *We'll see.*

When Bruce started telling Dad about his computer teacher my mind drifted. It would be great to have my own phone. I'd get a pink one with a really long cord so I could carry it from my desk to my night table. And I'd get a name number so my friends could just dial 662-STPH, the way you can dial 662-PIES when you want to order a pizza.

"So what do you think, Steph?" Dad asked.

"What?"

"She wasn't listening," Bruce said. "Her mind was someplace else."

"I was talking about our weekend plans," Dad said, "about staying at a hotel in the city. I thought we'd get out early to see the windows on Fifth Avenue. You know how crowded it gets over Thanksgiving. Then we could head up to the Museum of Natural History . . . and maybe to the Metropolitan . . . see a play on Saturday night . . ."

"That sounds great!" I said. "I didn't know we were going to the city for the weekend."

"That's because you were busy daydreaming," Bruce said.

"I wasn't daydreaming," I told him. "I was thinking."

"That's enough!" Dad said. "All that matters is that we have a good time together. And that means no fighting."

"We hardly ever fight anymore," Bruce told Dad.

"Well, that's good news," Dad said.

I wished I could call Rachel and Alison that minute and tell them about our plans, but Alison had already left for Sadie Wishnik's and Rachel had gone to her aunt's house, in New Hampshire.

As soon as we got home Bruce ran for the bathroom. Dr. Klaff says he has a small bladder. So if he drinks a lot he has to pee a lot. And he had two glasses of water plus a Coke at dinner. Dad says when he was a kid he had the same problem.

"See you tomorrow," Dad said, kissing my cheek.

"What do you mean, tomorrow?" I asked.

"I'm driving down to the city now. I've got a meeting first thing in the morning."

"You've got a meeting on Thanksgiving morning?"

"Yes," Dad said, "a breakfast meeting. It's the only time we could get together. But I'll be back in plenty of time for dinner."

"What about Mom?" I asked.

"What about her?"

"She's **going** to be so disappointed. You two haven't seen each other since summer."

"Did she tell you that?"

"Not exactly," I said.

"She knows about my meeting," Dad said. "And she's going to be busy with Thanksgiving dinner."

"Not that busy!"

"Don't worry about it . . . okay?" Dad kissed me again, this time on top of my head. "I'll be here tomorrow by two, at the latest."

Bruce had a nightmare that night. I heard him calling for Mom. I heard Mom padding down the hall to his room. I heard her talking softly to him. I guess I must have fallen right back asleep because when I opened my eyes again it was morning and I could smell the turkey roasting.

22

T-Day

Dad drove Carla and Katie up from the city. They got here before two, just as Dad had promised. Carla is tall and thin with wispy blonde hair. She wears suede and leather clothes, even in summer, and silver jewelry.

"Stephanie . . . look at you!" she said. Her voice was breathy, making her sound as if she'd just run around the block. "Aren't you something!" When she hugged me I could smell her perfume. Then she reached into her bag for a Kleenex and blew her nose. Mom says Carla developed allergies right after her husband died. She sneezes all year round.

"Can I help in the kitchen?" Carla asked Mom.

"Everything's ready," Mom said, wiping her hands on her jeans, "except me."

"I'll keep you company while you get dressed," Carla said.

"Will you watch the turkey, Steve?" Mom asked. "It needs basting every fifteen minutes."

"No problem," Dad said.

"Come on," Bruce said, grabbing Dad's hand and dragging him toward the den. "The game's on . . ."

Katie stood watching as everyone went off in different directions. She's small for eight, with chubby pink cheeks. She reminds me of a Cabbage Patch Kid. "You want to see my room?" I asked her.

"Sure."

We went upstairs. "This is nice," Katie said, looking around. "I like your posters. How come that one's on the ceiling?"

"That's my boyfriend," I told her.

"What's his name?"

"Benjamin."

"That's a nice name. How old is he?"

"Seventeen."

"That's really old. Are you going steady?"

"Yes, but my family doesn't know so don't say anything, okay?"

"Okay."

I took a deck of cards out of my desk drawer. "I'll teach you to play Spit."

"I already know how."

"You do?" That surprised me because I had never heard of the game until Alison taught me. "You want to play?" I asked her.

"Sure," she said.

Katie was really fast. She beat me twice before the rest of our guests arrived. They all came at once.

Aunt Robin and her live-in, Scott, brought their poodle, Enchilada. Gran Lola calls Enchilada her granddog. Aunt Robin and Scott are investment bankers. Their hobby is money. That's all they ever talk about. So they were extremely interested when I told Gran Lola and Papa Jack about my three stocks and how I came to choose them. "I picked Jiffy Lube because I liked the name, Revlon because Mom uses their makeup and Reebok because everybody wants to wear their shoes. So far I'm doing all right."

Uncle Richard, who is married to Aunt Denise, said that from his experience with the stock market, my reasons for choosing Revlon, Jiffy Lube and Reebok seemed as good as any.

At four we sat down to dinner. Everyone oohed and aahed as Mom carried in the turkey and set it in front of Dad. Then she took her seat at the opposite end of the table.

"Breast or leg?" Dad asked each of us as he carved the turkey.

"Breast!" Bruce called out and he and Katie started laughing.

"Oh, to be ten again," Cousin Stanley said, sighing, as if he were ninety years old instead of nineteen.

Papa Jack took his ulcer medicine before he ate anything.

After the main course Howard burped three times. "An excellent meal," he said, patting his middle.

During dessert a piece of pumpkin pie fell to the floor. Enchilada gobbled it up. I don't know if anyone besides me noticed. But a few minutes later Enchilada threw up on Bruce's shoe. Bruce took it personally. "These are my only shoes," he said. "What am I supposed to wear to school on Monday? If I wear these all the kids will hold their noses and say, *Yuck . . . barf!*"

"Take them off and put them in the laundry room," Mom said. When Bruce didn't move she added, "Hurry up!"

Aunt Robin took Enchilada outside, just in case, while Scott cleaned up under the table. "You'd be better off with a baby," Gran Lola said, when Aunt Robin came back. "A baby isn't any more trouble than that dog."

"Babies grow up," Aunt Robin said, looking at Howard.

Howard burped.

Papa Jack took some more ulcer medicine.

By eight, our company had left, including Carla and Katie, who drove back to the city with Aunt Robin and Scott. Suddenly the house seemed very quiet. The four of us cleared the table. Then Mom loaded the dishwasher and Dad scrubbed the pots and pans, while I wrapped the leftovers. I guess Mom and Dad were too tired to talk.

When I finished I went upstairs to change because I'd dropped a blob of cranberry sauce on my shirt. While I was in my room Dad poked his head in and said, "If you hurry and pack we can still get down to the city tonight."

"I didn't know we were going tonight."

"Yes."

"But Mom has to work in the morning, doesn't she?"

"Stephanie," Dad said, "sit down."

There are times when you know you're going to hear something that you don't want to hear. Something that you've kept yourself from thinking. I sat on the edge of my bed, chewing on the insides of my cheeks.

Dad paced the room. Finally he sat beside me. "I know you've guessed by now . . ."

"Guessed what?"

"About Mom and me . . . about our separation."

"What separation?"

"This separation," Dad said, sounding impatient. "About how we're living apart for a while."

"No!"

"I thought you knew," Dad said, shaking his head.

"What am I supposed to be . . . some kind of mind-reader?"

"But all those questions last night . . ." Dad said.

"What about them?"

Dad stood up. "Wait here . . ."

He went into the hall and called, "Row . . . would you come upstairs for a minute?"

I looked at Benjamin Moore. I forced myself to concentrate on him. If he were really my boyfriend I'd be getting ready to go out with him now. Probably we'd go to a movie first, then to Arcudi's for a pizza. While we were eating, Jeremy Dragon would come in with some of his friends and say, *Hey, Macbeth . . . how's it going?* Then I'd introduce him to Benjamin and he'd be really impressed, not just because Benjamin is so cute but because he's seventeen. Later, Jeremy would take me aside and ask for my phone number. I'd say, *Just dial 662-STPH.*

I heard Mom and Dad walk down the hall. I heard the rise and fall of their voices but I couldn't make out what they were saying. What exactly had Dad meant by a separation? And why had he acted as if it were my fault that I hadn't known all about it? I tiptoed down the hall. The door to Mom's room was closed. I stood outside and listened.

Dad said, "I thought we agreed not to hide it."

Mom said, "I wasn't hiding anything. They never asked. *I* thought we agreed that if they didn't seem concerned we wouldn't bring up the subject."

Then Dad said, "Well, the cat's out of the bag . . . and Stephanie's upset."

"Who's fault is that?" Mom asked.

And Dad said, "How was I supposed to know she really didn't have a clue . . ."

That did it! I threw open the door and shouted, "I suppose now you think I'm gullible!" I could see the look of surprise on their faces. "Well, I'm not. I can't be easily tricked by you or by anyone else!" I turned, slammed the door and ran back to my room where I threw myself face down on my bed.

"What's going on?" Bruce asked, standing in my doorway.

"Plenty," I told him. "And none of it's good!"

23

Weekend

I refused to go to New York with Dad. Bruce went without me.

"Don't you think you're being hard on him, Steph?" Mom said on Friday morning.

"Is that supposed to be a joke?" I asked, wolfing down my second bowl of cereal. "In case you're wondering," I added between mouthfuls, "I'm just as mad at you as I am at Dad."

"I can see that," Mom said, "and I'm sorry. I should have talked to you about the separation before but you seemed so happy . . . enjoying school and your friends . . ."

"So you let me go right on thinking that everything is the same as always."

"Well, in a way it is," Mom said. "Your life isn't going to change."

"How can you say that?"

"It's no different from when Dad's on a business trip, is it?"

"Until last night it wasn't any different." I cut myself a slice of apple pie and heated it in the microwave. "I suppose that's why we sold the yellow house and moved here," I said, "because of the separation."

"That's one reason."

"And I suppose everyone in the family knows."

"My sisters do," Mom said, "and Gran Lola and Papa Jack."

"And Carla?"

"Yes, Carla knows."

I finished my pie and stomped out of the room, leaving my dirty dishes on the table.

"Where are you going?" Mom called after me.

"Back to bed," I told her.

"I wish you'd get dressed and come to the office with me."

"No, thank you." I went upstairs and got into bed, pulling the quilt over my head.

When I woke up, two hours later, I heard Mom talking on the phone. Now that was really unusual because she never takes off from work. When one of us is sick and has to stay home from school, she gets Mrs. Greco to come in for the day.

I went to the kitchen and ate the leftover sweet potato pudding. All of it. I might have spaced out in front of the TV then, but Mom was still on the phone in the den. I couldn't tell if it was a business call or if she was blabbing to Aunt Denise, because when she saw me standing there, she covered the mouthpiece with her hand and waved me away. So I went back to bed. I slept on and off, all afternoon.

Mom looked in on me twice. The second time she felt my forehead, but I didn't let on that I knew.

By dinnertime I still hadn't gotten dressed. I went downstairs. Mom was on the phone again. "I'm going to eat now," I told her. This time she held up her hand, motioning for me to wait, but I didn't. I made myself a gigantic turkey sandwich on bread sliced so thick I could hardly fit it into my mouth. I ate half the left-over stuffing and the last piece of apple pie. Then I went back to bed.

On Saturday morning Mom came to my room. "As soon as you're dressed I'll drive you down to the station. Dad's waiting for you . . . he doesn't want you to miss the windows on Fifth Avenue."

"I'm not going anywhere," I said.

"He's got three tickets for a musical tonight."

"Let him take someone else," I said. Then I burped. I didn't meant to. It just slipped out.

"I know how much you like musicals, Steph . . ."

"I am *not* going to New York!"

Mom stayed home again and worked on the computer. That afternoon she found me in the kitchen, gnawing on a turkey leg. "Stuffing yourself isn't the answer," she said. "You're going to get sick if you keep this up."

"It's all your fault," I said.

"What do you mean?" Mom asked.

"I mean, if you weren't such a go-getter this wouldn't be happening. If we had all gone to California you and Dad wouldn't be separated now."

"That's not true," Mom said. "I don't know where you got such an idea."

"Then explain it to me," I said, searching the refrigerator for the jar of dill pickles.

Mom closed the refrigerator door and stood blocking it. "Dad and I have some problems. We're trying to work them out."

"What problems?"

Mom sighed. "He's bored with his life. He wants to make changes. I like my life the way it is . . ."

"But he *had* to go to California," I said. "He had no choice."

"He *asked* to go to California," Mom said.

"I don't believe you!" I said. "I don't think you even care about this separation. If you did you'd be crying!"

"When I feel like crying I do it in private," Mom said, raising her voice. "I don't tell you everything."

For a minute neither one of us spoke. Then Mom softened. "Look," she began, trying to put her arm around me. I jumped out of the way. I wasn't about to let her touch me. "We're not going to make any hasty decisions . . . I can promise you that. This is just a trial separation."

"How long does a trial separation last?" I asked.

"As long as necessary," Mom said.

I ate a piece of pumpkin pie without even tasting it.

That night, when I went to bed *again*, I thought over what Mom had said about Dad being bored with his life. I don't understand how he could be bored. He's got a wonderful family. He's got a good job. He makes enough money. Maybe what he needs is a hobby, I thought. Maybe he needs to get interested in something like scuba diving or refinishing furniture. Or maybe he's having his mid-life crisis. Yes, that's probably it! When Rachel's father had his mid-life crisis, a few years ago, he changed his job. He used to be a lawyer and now he's a teacher. Maybe Dad should become a teacher, too. Then he could get a job at the high school, like Mr. Robinson. He could even coach football since that's his favorite sport. And that way he wouldn't have to commute to the city or fly away on business trips. I fell asleep wondering what subject Dad should teach.

I slept until noon on Sunday. When I got up I threw on a pair of jeans and a sweatshirt. Then I hit the kitchen. I polished off the rest of the pumpkin pie, the stuffing and most of the turkey. I was beginning to feel like I might explode. I needed to get out of the house. I put on my new winter jacket, the one I got two weeks ago. Mom wanted me to buy it in either red or blue but I held out for purple. I zipped it up and went out the back door. It was cold out, and gray. Winter was definitely coming. I burped twice. Too bad Howard wasn't there. He'd have been proud of me.

The wind whipped around my head, hurting my ears. I covered them with my hands and kicked stones as I walked down to the pond. When I got there I sat on a log, facing the water. I sat until my feet were numb from the cold. Then I jumped up and down trying to get the feeling back in my toes. But that made the food slosh around in my stomach and I started to feel sick. I grabbed a handful of stones and tossed them one by one, into the pond, hoping to get them to skim the water. But none of them did. Then I sat on the log again.

I don't know how long I'd been sitting there when I saw Dad's rental car. It slowed down, stopped briefly, and Bruce jumped out. "Hey, Steph . . ." he called, running toward me. "What are you doing?"

"What does it look like I'm doing?" I asked.

"Sitting by the pond and freezing your butt."

"Very good."

"We had a great time in New York. We saw the best show."

"What show?"

"*Little Shop of Horrors.*"

"I saw the movie."

"Yeah . . . but the show was better. It was so funny." He imitated Audrey II, the talking plant. "Feed me, Seymour . . . feed me!"

I almost laughed.

"Dad gave your ticket to Carla."

"Carla took *my* ticket?"

"Yes . . . and she liked the show a lot."

"That's disgusting!" I said.

"What is?"

"That Dad would give my ticket to Carla and that she would take it!"

Bruce shrugged. "What'd you do all weekend?"

"I did nothing . . . that's what!"

"Oh." He picked up a stone and tossed it. It

skimmed along the water. "Let's go home now, okay? Dad wants to talk to you before he leaves."

"I'm staying here until he's gone."

"But . . ."

"Why don't you go tell him that for me?" I shivered and hugged myself, trying to keep warm.

Bruce reached into his pocket and pulled out a ski hat. "Here," he said, dropping it in my lap. Then he ran up the hill to our house.

My eyes filled with tears. I sniffled and checked my pockets for a tissue to blow my nose. But the pockets were empty. I pulled on Bruce's hat.

A few minutes later Dad parked his car by the side of the road. "Steph . . ." he called, waving for me to join him.

I acted like I didn't even notice.

So Dad came down to the pond. "We missed you this weekend," he said, sitting beside me on the log.

I didn't say anything.

He picked up a stick and began scratching the ground with it. "I'm sorry you found out the way you did. Mom and I should have told you sooner."

I still didn't respond.

"Look . . ." he said, "I just want you to know that no matter what happens I'll always be your father."

"Did you read that in some book?" I asked.

"Some book that tells you how to talk to your kids when you're separating because you're bored with your life?"

"I didn't read it anywhere," Dad said. "It's how I feel. And who told you I was bored with my life?"

"Mom . . . who do you think?" A squirrel ran in front of us. I watched him for a minute, then I looked over at Dad. "Is it true?"

"I suppose it is in some ways . . ." Dad said. "But it has nothing to do with you or Bruce."

"Does it have to do with Mom?"

"Not with Mom exactly . . . but with the direction of our marriage."

"And all this time I thought you *had* to go to California." I practically spit out those words.

"We needed time apart . . . to think things through . . ."

"So how come you couldn't think in Connecticut or New York? How come you had to go across the country to think?"

"It seemed easier at the time." He glanced at his watch. "I've got a plane to catch."

"Planes are more important than families, right?"

He sucked in his breath but he didn't deny it. "I want you and Bruce to come out to L.A. over Christmas," he said. "We'll have more time to talk then." He leaned over to kiss me but I pulled away from him. "You're making this very hard, Steph."

"Good," I told him.

Rachel called that night. "Our weekend was a disaster!" she said. "My brother was so obnoxious . . . he had Mom and Jessica in tears . . . Dad lost his temper . . . and finally, Charles stormed out of my aunt's house and went to stay with friends. I don't know why he has to be so impossible. I don't know why he can't get along with us. Anyway, I can't think of a worse Thanksgiving!" She paused to catch her breath. "So how was yours?"

"Great."

"How was your father?"

"Great."

"What'd you do?"

"We ate a lot."

Rachel laughed. "Did you go to the city?"

"No."

"I thought you would."

"No time."

"When will your father be back?"

"He's not sure."

"For Christmas?"

"Probably."

"Well . . . the time between Thanksgiving and Christmas always goes fast."

"Yeah . . . right."

"Oh, I almost forget," Rachel said, "I made All-State Orchestra."

"You did?"

"Yes. The letter was waiting for me when I got home. Stacey Green made it, too. We're going to be really busy with rehearsals. In April there's a concert. You'll come, won't you?"

"Sure."

"Well . . . I'm glad you had a good weekend."

"Yeah. See you tomorrow."

An hour later Alison called. "Hi . . . I'm home."

"How was your Thanksgiving?" I asked.

"Leon and Sadie had a fight."

"How could anybody fight with Sadie?"

"She says Leon's the only one who ever does."

"I thought he's so proud of her."

"Yeah, but see . . . Sadie's friends are always dropping off manuscripts for Leon to read. They all know somebody who's trying to write. But Leon can't stand to look at other people's work. So he tells Sadie, *If I wanted to do that I'd be a teacher instead of a writer.* So then Sadie says, *What will I tell my friends?* So then Leon says, *Tell them your son is a selfish man who guards his free time.* So then Sadie says, *My friends will be very disappointed.*

So then Leon blows up and tells Sadie she has no understanding of his work. Then he slams out of the house, Sadie winds up in tears and Mom locks herself in the bedroom and won't come out. It was all very depressing."

"Was this before Thanksgiving dinner or after?"

"After. Sadie didn't show him the manuscripts until Friday night."

"That was smart. So did they finally make up or what?"

"Yes, but not until Saturday morning." She paused. "So how was your weekend?"

"Great!"

"Well, I'm glad somebody had a great time."

Later, as I came out of the bathroom on my way to bed, Bruce called to me from his room. "What?" I asked, standing in his doorway.

He was sitting up in bed with the atlas in his lap. "Dad says I should pretend he's on a business trip. He says it's just a trial separation."

I walked over and sat on the edge of his bed. The atlas was opened to a map of California. "Did he tell you what that means?"

"It means they live apart and think things over."

"Did he tell you anything else?"

"No . . . except we're going to L.A. over Christmas. Would you rather go to Marineland, Disneyland or Universal Pictures?"

"I may not go at all," I said.

"Then I'm not going either." He closed the atlas, looking very sad.

"We don't have to decide yet," I said, in my most cheerful voice. "And I think pretending he's on a business trip is a good idea. I think we should both do that . . . because before you know it, they'll probably be back together. I'll bet they're back together by my birthday." I could see that made Bruce feel better so I kept going. "You know Miri Levine . . . this girl in my class? Well, her parents got divorced when we were in fourth grade and when we were in sixth . . . they got married again . . . to each other."

"Really?" Bruce asked.

"Yes. So let's not say anything to our friends about this separation or we'll just have to explain all over again when they get back together."

"You don't think they'll get divorced?" Bruce asked.

"No! Who's talking about divorce?"

"I think I'll go to sleep now," Bruce said. "Tell Mom I'm ready for my kiss, okay?" He snuggled down under his quilt.

"Good night," I said.

As I was leaving he called, "Steph . . ."

"Yeah?"

"It wasn't that much fun in New York without you."

"I'm not surprised." I danced out of his room singing, "Feed me, Seymour . . . feed me."

I got into bed feeling a lot better. It's funny how when you try to help somebody else feel better you wind up feeling better yourself.

24

Peter Klaff

At school everything was the same, except that
Jeremy Dragon was wearing a winter jacket. On
Monday morning we had a fire drill before first
period. On the way back to homeroom Peter
Klaff told me he'd had two warts removed from
his middle finger over the holiday weekend.

"Did your mother do it?" I asked.

"Yeah . . . with dry ice," Peter said. "It burned."
He held his finger up to my face. "You see that
. . . right there . . . that's where they were."

Peter Klaff had never stood so close to me. I
pretended to be really interested in the black
marks on the back of his finger. I even touched
them, just to show how interested I was. Peter is
growing. He comes up past my eyes now. "It

must be weird having your mother for your doctor."

As soon as I said that I got a mental picture of the Klaff family sitting around their dinner table. I could hear Dr. Klaff saying, *Stephanie Hirsch was in for her yearly check-up today. Her breasts are beginning to develop.*

It's about time, Peter would say, between mouthfuls.

She's probably going to get her period soon, Dr. Klaff would say, helping herself to more linguini.

I'm glad you mentioned that, Mom, Peter would say. *From now on I'll keep a look-out for anything red on the back of her pants.*

That's very thoughtful of you, Peter, Dr. Klaff would say. *So many boys your age act foolish about menstruation. Here, have some more bread.*

I must have had a strange expression on my face because Peter said, "What?"

"Nothing . . ." I said. "I was just wondering if your mother talks about her patients at home . . . like when you're sitting around the dinner table?"

"Nah . . . she talks about the Mets. She's a baseball fanatic."

"What about when baseball season's over . . . like now?"

"Movies," Peter said. "She's a movie fanatic, too."

"Oh . . ." I felt relieved. "I thought maybe she talks about diseases and stuff like that."

"Hardly ever," Peter said.

This was definitely the longest conversation we'd ever had. And I didn't want it to end yet. So I said, "Do you use apple shampoo?"

"Yeah . . . how did you know?"

"I can smell it," I said. "It smells nice."

He came even closer to me, stood on tiptoe, and sniffed my hair. "Yours smells nice, too. Like uh . . ."

"Almonds," I told him.

"Yeah . . . like almonds."

The next morning, when I got to homeroom, I found a small plastic bottle on my desk. On the side there was a picture of an apple. I opened it and sniffed what was inside. Apple shampoo! I looked over at Peter Klaff. We smiled at each other and I put the bottle in my bag. This was the first gift I'd ever had from a boy. I was glad Alison was busy talking to Miri Levine and that neither one of them had noticed the private look Peter and I shared.

The following morning Mrs. Remo was late getting to homeroom. While we were waiting to see if we'd have a substitute, Eric Macaulay told us a gross joke. Alison threw her shoe at him and said, "That is the sleaziest joke I've ever heard!"

Just as her shoe hit Eric's head Mrs. Remo came into the room.

"Really!" Mrs. Remo said. "This is not the kind of behavior I expect from my homeroom when I'm late. Alison and Stephanie . . . you can both report to me after school this afternoon."

I was shocked. First of all, I hadn't been doing anything wrong. Second of all, I'd never seen Mrs. Remo in such a bad mood.

We told Rachel about it at lunch. She couldn't believe it either. "Just because you threw your shoe at him?" she asked Alison.

"Yes," Alison said.

Then I said, "And when Alison tried to explain that I didn't have anything to do with it, Mrs. Remo said, *Maybe next time you'll think before you act.* Now what does that have to do with anything?" I asked Rachel. "I mean, does that make any sense to you?"

"No," Rachel said.

"She's been acting that way since we came back from Thanksgiving," Alison said.

"Maybe she didn't have a good holiday," Rachel suggested.

"Probably plenty of people didn't have a good holiday," Alison said.

I didn't say anything. I just unwrapped my lunch and started to eat.

On Thursday night I was in the pantry with the phone, talking to Alison and finishing off a bag of oatmeal cookies. As soon as I hung up, the phone rang again. I picked it up, expecting Rachel or maybe Alison, who sometimes forgets to tell me something and has to call back. But it was Peter Klaff. He asked for our math assignment. I gave it to him. Then he said, "Thank you very much," and he hung up.

I couldn't believe it. Peter Klaff calling me! How come he didn't ask his sister, Kara, for the assignment? She's also in our math class. There must have been more to his call than math.

Later, Dad called, but I refused to speak to him. "Tell him I'm in the shower," I said to Bruce.

Before I went to sleep I *did* take a shower. And I washed my hair with Peter Klaff's apple shampoo. When I got into bed I looked up at Benjamin Moore. Peter's not a hunk, like Benjamin. And he's not as sexy as Jeremy Dragon. But for a seventh grade boy, he's okay. I think I might decide to like him.

25

The
Sharing Season

The symphonic band is playing for the Christmas-Hanukkah show. It's an original musical called *The Sharing Season*, about a modern couple named Mary and Joe who come from different religious backgrounds. They want their kids to understand and respect both holidays so they take turns telling them about Christmas and Hanukkah.

Dana Carpenter is playing Mary and Jeremy Dragon is playing Joe so I'm very glad I'm in symphonic band. On the first day of rehearsals I couldn't take my eyes off Jeremy. That's why I missed my cue and Ms. Lopez had to stop the symphonic band. "We should have had a drum roll there," she said. "Let's try to stay awake on the snare drum, please." I was so embarrassed!

After a week of rehearsals Dana and Jeremy started acting as if they really *were* Mary and Joe. Instead of hanging out in the back of the school bus with his friends, Jeremy sat up front with Dana now. And in the halls at school they held hands and looked at each other like sick dogs. I wondered if she knew he had hairy legs.

I was so busy at school I didn't have time to think about my parents. But sometimes, when I least expected it, I'd get a gnawing pain in my stomach or my leg would start twitching. That's what happened in the locker room today, while we were getting changed for gym. I sat down on the bench and rubbed my leg.

"What's wrong?" Rachel asked.

"Nothing."

Rachel stepped into her gym shorts and tucked her shirt inside. "Maybe you're getting your period."

"What does my leg have to do with getting my period?"

Alison didn't wait for Rachel to answer. "How come you never tell me I'm getting *my* period?" she asked Rachel.

"Steph is more developed than you," Rachel said.

"I've been eating a lot of bananas," Alison said.

"Bananas?" Rachel repeated.

"I heard bananas put weight on you fast," Alison said. "And if I gain weight maybe I'll grow on top . . . and if I grow on top . . ."

"How old was your mother when she got it?" Rachel asked.

"Gena was twelve," Alison said.

"Because these things are basically inherited," Rachel continued.

"Oh . . ." Alison said. "I have no idea how old my biological mother was."

"But she must have had it by the time she was fifteen," I told Alison, "because that's when she had you . . . right?"

Alison nodded.

I stood up. My leg had stopped twitching.

"I still think you're getting your period," Rachel said.

"I promise when I do you'll be the first to know."

"What about me?" Alison asked.

"You'll be the first *two* to know . . . okay?"

"Okay," they both said.

On Saturday afternoon the three of us were at Rachel's, discussing Dana and Jeremy.

"It's obvious they're in love," Alison said.

"If he has to be in love with a ninth grade girl I'm glad it's Dana," I said.

"Me too," Rachel added. "At least she's smart."

"Yes, but I wish she'd stop humming under her breath at the bus stop." I stretched out on the floor with a bag of potato chips.

"No crumbs, please," Rachel said.

"You're so fusty!" I learned that word from her.

"I think you mean fussy," Rachel said, "because *fusty* means either *musty* or *old-fashioned*."

"Then you're fussy," I said, shoveling the chips into my mouth.

"Better to be fussy than slovenly," Rachel said.

"I'm not exactly slovenly," I said. "I'm just not as perfect as you."

"I'm not perfect," Rachel said. "I'm just organized."

"I wouldn't mind being half as organized," Alison said. She circled the room, running her hand over the row of framed pictures on Rachel's dresser, the tray of miniature perfume bottles, the collection of painted jars and boxes.

Sometimes, when Alison is at Rachel's she'll stare at the clothes in her closet, admiring the way everything faces the same direction. "I'll bet you never have trouble finding anything," she'll say.

"Never," Rachel will answer.

Alison ran her hand across the books on Rachel's shelves, arranged in alphabetical order by the author's last name. "Oh . . . I read this one," she said, taking down a copy of *Life With Father*. "It was funny."

"Yeah," I said, "but if it were written today it would probably be called *Life Without Father*." I forced a laugh at my own joke. Rachel and Alison looked at me. "I mean," I said, trying to explain, "so many fathers have to travel for their jobs."

Alison nodded. "I'm so glad Leon doesn't have to travel." She put the book back on the shelf. "Speaking of travels . . . we're going back to our house in California for Christmas."

"Really?" I said. "My father wants us to come out over Christmas, too."

"Maybe you can visit me in Malibu," Alison said.

"You're both going to be gone over Christmas?" Rachel asked. "You're both deserting me?"

"Stacey Green will be around, won't she?" I asked.

"I don't know," Rachel said. "She's not the same kind of friend as you. She's a music friend, that's all."

"But she slept over last weekend, didn't she?" I asked.

"Yes, because we had rehearsals for All-State."

"It's just for two weeks," Alison told her.

"Two weeks!" Rachel cried. "Did you know that Christmas vacation is the time when more people get seriously depressed than any other time of the year? And it's because they have no one special to share their holidays!" Her voice broke.

No one spoke for a minute, then Alison said, "I'm going to ask my mom if you can come to Malibu with us."

"I couldn't possibly leave my family at holiday time," Rachel told her. "They need me." Then she made a small noise, almost like a yelp, and ran out of the room, hands over her face. We heard the door to the bathroom close and lock. Then we heard Rachel crying.

Alison and I looked at each other. "She's very sensitive, isn't she?"

"Yes . . . and it was really nice of you to invite her," I said.

"Even so . . . I feel bad. I shouldn't have said anything about you visiting me in Malibu."

"She'll be okay."

"I hope so."

Mom isn't coming to L.A. with Bruce and me. She's going to Venice, Italy. She says it will be hard to be away from us but she's always wanted to see Venice and this is the perfect opportunity because a group of travel agents are going together. She seems excited about her trip, a lot more excited than I am about mine.

I haven't talked to Dad on the phone since Thanksgiving. I get tense when he calls. I always ask Bruce to make excuses for me. But when the phone rang on Sunday night I answered without thinking and it was him.

"You've certainly been busy lately," he said.

"Yes." My palms were sweaty. I reminded myself that this was my father. There was no reason to panic just because he was on the other end of the phone.

"How's the weather?" he asked.

"Sunny but very cold."

"What are you doing in school?"

"Rehearsing for the holiday show. Too bad you won't be here to see it."

"I wish I could be."

"I'll bet."

"Stephanie . . ."

"I really have to go now," I told him. "I'll get Bruce."

Mom came to my room later. I was lying on my bed, staring up at Benjamin Moore. "I overheard part of your conversation with Dad," she said, "and I think I should set the record straight.

You're blaming him for something that's not entirely his fault."

"I thought you said it was all his idea."

"Going to California . . . yes. But I wanted this separation, too. I just wasn't willing to initiate it. Dad forced it out into the open. Probably, in the long run, that's good."

"I'm glad you both like the idea so much!"

The next night, when Mom came home from work, she dropped a bag on my bed. "I was passing the sports store and they were having a special on Speedo bathing suits. I thought you might need one for L.A."

I think Mom's noticed that I've gained weight. I've been using a safety pin to hold my jeans together and wearing big shirts over them to hide the evidence. My gym shorts are getting tight but they have an elastic waistband so I can still squeeze into them.

I tried on the bathing suit. It was blue, with a diagonal white stripe. I looked terrible in it. I looked fat.

The Sharing Season was a big success. Mom and Bruce came to the evening performance and after it, Rachel and Alison came back to our house. It was our last chance to exchange holiday presents before vacation began. Our gifts to each other all turned out to be purple. We hadn't planned it that way. It just happened. I guess it's because purple is our favorite color.

I gave Alison and Rachel sets of barrettes, hand-painted with little purple flowers. Rachel gave us each purple T-shirts that said *FRIENDS* and Alison gave us purple leather picture frames. Inside was a photo of the three of us, plus Maizie, Burt and Harry. Leon had taken the picture right before Thanksgiving. We'd had to carry Burt and Harry to Alison's in their cage, the one the Robinsons use to take them to the vet. In the picture we're sitting on Alison's bed, laughing our heads off. Alison is holding Maizie, Rachel is holding Burt and I'm holding Harry, who is trying to escape. It's a great picture.

But when Rachel looked at it she started to cry. "I'm going to die of loneliness without the two of you!" That got Alison started and a minute later, I was in tears, too.

Finally Mom came to my room and asked if everything was all right. We explained that it was and Mom asked if we'd like a pizza. Of course we said "Yes."

While we were waiting I taught Rachel and Alison a song I'd learned at camp. It's called *Side by Side*. The part I like best goes:

Through all kinds of weather
What if the sky should fall
Just as long as we're together
It doesn't matter at all

We sang it about twenty times, until we were laughing so hard we had to stop.

26

Iris

Dear Rachel,

Well, here I am in sunny California! It's so weird
here! It smells like summer but there are Christmas decorations everywhere. You can sit on the
deck of Dad's apartment and watch the volleyball
games on the beach. And there's a marina with
hundreds of boats just a block away. Bruce likes
to hang out there with his new friend, Shirley.
Shirley is visiting her father, who's divorced.
She's ten, same as Bruce. I'm glad Bruce has
found a friend here because now I am free to do
whatever I want and there's just so much to
do . . .

I went on for three pages in my letter to Rachel
but I didn't tell her the real truth except for the

description of Dad's place. I didn't tell her how unhappy I was feeling or how homesick, or how Bruce has been having nightmares. We were sleeping next to each other on rollaway beds in the living room. So every night I'd get up with him and comfort him until he fell back to sleep.

I didn't tell Rachel that it wasn't always sunny here, that sometimes it was damp and foggy and the ocean was freezing and nobody in his right mind would get wet. I didn't tell her that Mom wasn't with us. And I certainly didn't tell her about Iris.

Iris is Dad's friend. That's how he'd introduced her to us on our first night in California. "Kids . . . this is my friend, Iris. She lives down the hall. We met in the laundry room."

"I've heard a lot about you," Iris said.

"I haven't heard a word about you," I answered.

Before we went out to dinner that night Dad looked me over and said, "Wow, Steph . . . you've really been putting it on."

I was hoping he would add something else. Something like, *But you still look great to me!* When he didn't, I said, "I haven't gained an ounce. You've just forgotten what I look like."

Then Iris said, "Maybe you could come to exercise class with me. I go every day at four."

"That's a fine idea," Dad said.

"I have other plans," I told them both. Right away I could tell it was going to be a long two weeks.

I suppose it could be worse. Iris could look like one of those girls on the beach who are always playing volleyball. They're tall and tan and skinny with long blonde hair and they say *Hi* as if it's a six syllable word. But Iris is small with short dark hair and pale, creamy skin. She isn't even young. She's thirty-six. She's divorced but she doesn't have any kids. I knew from the start that Dad and Iris weren't just friends. I knew from the way they looked at each other— the same way Dana and Jeremy do—like sick dogs.

Iris works for an entertainment agency. Her job is finding books that would make good movies. It sounds like a really easy job to me. All she has to do is read. But over the holidays she was reading at home instead of at the office. Except *home* seemed to mean Dad's place. After a couple of days I'd asked Dad, "Doesn't Iris have any other friends?"

"Sure," Dad said. He was also taking time off from the office.

"Then how come she's always hanging around here?"

"I think her other friends are away for the holidays."

"What about family?" I asked. "Doesn't she have any family?"

"No," Dad said, "she doesn't."

I thought about what Rachel had told us. About how people can get very depressed during the holidays if they don't have friends or family. So I didn't say anything else about Iris hanging around. Not then, anyway.

I decided the only way to get through the two weeks was by telling Dad I had a lot of school work to do. "Tons of reading," is how I put it. Dad and Iris were impressed, which meant they left me alone.

I still hadn't worn the bathing suit Mom bought for me. Nobody thought that was strange because Iris doesn't wear a bathing suit either. She says she's allergic to the sun. I told her that's a real coincidence, because so am I. When Iris does sit outside she wears a wide-brimmed straw hat. The only makeup she uses is lip gloss, which she carries around in her pocket and smears on her lips at least a hundred times a day. I wonder if Dad gets it on his face when they kiss. I hate to think of them kissing! But I'm sure they do. Iris is always touching Dad. She touches him a lot more than he touches her but I haven't heard him complaining. I wonder if Mom knows about her.

We were eating out every night at medium

fancy restaurants where I ordered huge dinners and finished every mouthful. "You certainly have a healthy appetite," Iris said one night.

"Yes," I said, "isn't Dad lucky . . . suppose he had a daughter with anorexia instead?"

"Mmm . . ." Iris said. She says that a lot.

Everyone around here is thin. Everyone except me. Well, who cares! Since I've been here I eat as much as I feel like eating, whenever I feel like eating.

After dinner, we'd usually play a game of Scrabble and I'd eat either ice cream or cookies, depending on what I'd had for dessert at the restaurant. I'm getting good at Scrabble. Once I scored thirty-two points on the word *fusty*. Iris asked if I knew what it meant. "Yes," I told her. It has two meanings—one is *musty* and the other is *old-fashioned*. She couldn't believe I knew so much.

Yesterday, Dad took Bruce on a fishing trip. The boat left at five AM. Dad wanted me to come, too, but I said, "No, thanks." I don't like the idea of fishing. It's bloody and disgusting. I was really shocked that Bruce wanted to go. After all, fishing is a violent act. But I didn't discuss that with him. I was afraid if I did he'd have more nightmares, about fish getting nuked.

"If you won't come with us I'll ask Iris to keep you company," Dad said.

"I don't need a babysitter," I told him.

"Iris won't mind. And the two of you can spend the day reading."

There was no point in arguing.

I slept until ten that morning. And when I got up Iris was already there, reading on the deck. I heard her radio. She plays classical music all the time. In some ways she reminds me of Rachel, like the way she reads a book a day and the kind of music she enjoys. I wonder if Rachel will be like Iris when she grows up. I wonder if Iris and Rachel would get along if Iris were Mr. Robinson's friend.

I threw on my shorts and shirt and carried the container of orange juice out onto the deck.

"Good morning," Iris said.

"Morning," I answered, taking a swig of juice directly from the carton.

"Why don't you get a glass, Stephanie?" Iris said. "It's more sanitary that way."

"I don't mind," I said, taking another drink.

"I was thinking about the rest of us," Iris said.

I ignored that and wiped the juice off my mouth with the back of my hand. "So . . ." I said, "how long have you and Dad known each other?"

"About six weeks," she said. "We met in the

laundry room right before Thanksgiving." She smiled when she said that. She and Dad must think that meeting in the laundry room is really cute.

"We had a fabulous Thanksgiving," I told her. "Mom and Dad were so glad to see each other!" I drank from the carton again. "Dad was hoping Mom would come out here for the holidays but she had to go to Italy . . . on business."

I didn't wait for Iris's reaction. I went back inside and pulled my wallet out of my duffel bag. Then I went out to the deck again. "You want to see a picture of my mother?" I asked, flipping through the photos in my wallet. When I came to Mom's I flashed it in front of Iris's face. "Isn't she pretty?"

Iris studied the picture.

"She's got a very successful travel agency," I said. "She's a real go-getter . . . she makes a lot more money than Dad." I had no idea if that was true but it sounded good. "They've been married fifteen years," I added. "May twenty-fourth is their anniversary."

Iris marked her place in the book she'd been reading with a piece of Kleenex. Then she closed the book and rested it in her lap. "I know how you feel about me, Stephanie," she said, looking directly at me.

"No, you don't," I told her.

"Okay . . . maybe I don't know, exactly, but . . ."

"That's right. You don't know exactly."

"Well, you're making it pretty clear," Iris said.

I leaned over the railing of the deck and looked down. "My parents are trying to work out their problems," I told her, "and I don't think Dad can work his out with you hanging around night and day."

"Will you please watch what you're doing!" Iris said as I leaned over even farther.

I could taste the orange juice coming up. If I do fall, I thought, I probably won't die. I'll probably just break an arm or leg. We're only three stories up. "You're wasting your time if you think Dad's going to marry you," I said, "because this is just a trial separation which means you're just a trial girlfriend." I straightened up and sat in the canvas chair, opposite Iris, with my arms folded across my chest. "So why don't you go and find somebody else?"

Tears sprang to Iris's eyes. "You know, at first I wanted you to like me," she said, "but now I really don't care if you do or you don't." She jumped up. "Excuse me . . . I just remembered there's something I have to do at home."

"Take your time . . ." I called after her.

I spent the rest of the morning sitting in the

deck chair, looking out at the ocean, and wondering why I didn't feel better now that I'd told Iris my true feelings.

While I was eating lunch Alison called and asked me to come to Malibu either tomorrow or the next day. I told her I couldn't.

Alison was disappointed. "Mom says she'll send a car for you so your folks won't have to make the trip."

"I wish I could," I said, "but . . ."

"Are you trying to tell me something?" Alison asked.

"What would I be trying to tell you?"

"That you're embarrassed to ride in a car with a driver?"

"No," I said.

"Are you embarrassed because you think we'll have a house full of movie stars?"

"No . . . I never even thought of that." Actually, a house full of movie stars sounded pretty good to me. And I'd love to see Alison's house. Most of all, I'd love to see Alison. But I just can't do it. I can't explain what's going on here. And I can't pretend that I'm having a great time when I'm not. Alison would know in a second that something is wrong.

"It's very quiet around here," Alison said. "Mom hasn't been feeling well so she's resting a lot."

"What's wrong with her?"

"Leon says she's exhausted from filming the series."

"That's too bad."

"I suppose I could come to your father's place."

"No," I said, quickly. "It's very crowded here and . . ."

"I guess you want to spend as much time as possible with him," Alison said.

"Yes."

"I understand," Alison said. "I'd feel the same way."

Just as I hung up the phone Iris came back. She didn't say a word. She just went out to the deck and settled in again, with her books and her radio.

I ran out of the apartment and down the outside stairs leading to the beach. Oh, I hated Iris! And I hated Dad for having her around when this was supposed to be our vacation! I walked along the ocean's edge for more than an hour. I came back full of sand, my eyes stinging from the salt air. I knew Iris would tell Dad what had happened between us so I spent the rest of the afternoon in the bathtub, planning my defense.

That night, instead of going out to dinner, Dad decided to cook the fish he and Bruce had caught.

"We don't like fish," I said.

"You've never had fish this fresh," Dad said.

"Does it have bones?"

"If you get one you just spit it out."

"I think I'll have tuna," I said.

"Tuna *is* fish," Dad said.

"But it's in a can," I told him. "And it doesn't have any bones."

"I'll have tuna, too," Bruce said.

Dad sighed. "You two don't know what you're missing. Maybe Iris will come over and help me eat this fish."

But Iris told Dad she thought she'd stay at home for a change. So Dad took some fish down the hall to her apartment. He was gone for an hour.

After dinner, instead of playing Scrabble, Dad called me into his room. He shut the door and said, "You were very rude to Iris today."

"I told her the truth," I said. "I told her that you and Mom are trying to work out your problems, which is what *you* told me."

"I expect you to treat my friends with respect, Stephanie."

"Respect has to be earned," I said.

"Where did you hear that?" he asked.

"I read it in one of Mom's books about raising kids."

"I see," Dad said.

"It wouldn't hurt you to read some of those books."

Dad raised his voice. "I don't need you telling me what to read!"

"I think I'll go home tomorrow," I said, my voice breaking. "I think I'll stay with Gran Lola until Mom gets back."

"You're not going home until January second," Dad said.

"We'll see!" I told him, turning on my heels.

He came up behind me and grabbed my arm. "You are *not* going home until the second!" he repeated.

I shook free of him. "What am I . . . a prisoner here?"

"Prisoners don't get to go to Disneyland," Dad said. "And that's where we're going tomorrow."

"Is Iris coming with us?"

"No . . . Iris has other plans."

"Too bad," I said as I left Dad's room. I went directly to the refrigerator and took out the jar of peanut butter. I've told Iris that we don't keep our peanut butter in the refrigerator but she doesn't listen. I opened the jar, stuck in my finger and dug out a cold blob. I put it in my mouth all at once. Then I got ready for bed.

On the plane going home, I said to Bruce, "Mom and Dad probably won't be back together by my birthday."

"I know," Bruce said. He was working one of those puzzles where you have to move small plastic tiles around until you get the numbers in the right order. Shirley's father gave it to him. "They're probably going to get divorced."

"They are not," I said.

"Then what about Iris?"

"Iris is just a fling."

"What's a fling?" he asked.

"A romance that doesn't last."

"How do you know?"

"Because I've read a lot of romances."

"Oh," Bruce said. "I hope you're right." He moved around a few more tiles, then he held the puzzle up for me to see. "Look at this . . . I got it!"

27

Reunion

I was so glad to get home! I called Alison, then Rachel. We made plans to get together that night, right after dinner. Rachel said she'd come to my house first, then we'd walk over to Alison's.

When Rachel rang the bell I answered the door. "Hi . . ." she said, "welcome home." She didn't shriek or jump up and down so neither did I.

As soon as Mom heard Rachel's voice she came into the hall and gave her a hug. "Happy New Year!"

"Happy New Year to you, too," Rachel said. "How was Venice?"

Mom glanced at me. "It was wonderful," she

said, slowly. "Of course it was hard to be away from the family . . ."

"I know what you mean," Rachel said. "I could never be away from my family over the holidays."

"Did Charles get home?" Mom asked.

"No, he went to visit a friend from school . . . in Florida."

"That's a good place to have a friend this time of year."

"I know."

"We're going over to Alison's now," I told Mom.

"Be back by eight-thirty," Mom said. "Tomorrow's a school day. And take your flashlight."

As soon as we were outside Rachel said, "Your father must have been really disappointed."

"About what?"

"That your mother went to Venice."

"Oh, yeah . . . but he understood. She had to go. It was a business trip."

"At least she had a nice time, though," Rachel said.

"Yeah." I shined the flashlight on my wrist. "Look what she brought me." I was wearing a bracelet made of something called Murano beads. Each one is a different color and decorated in a different way.

"It's pretty," Rachel said.

"Thanks."

"Did you and Alison see a lot of each other in California?" Rachel asked.

"No."

"How come?"

"No time," I explained.

"But you at least got to her house in Malibu . . . right?"

"No . . . we never got together at all."

"What?" Rachel said. "I can't believe it!"

"I know."

"But why?"

"I told you . . . no time. My father had so many plans. Fishing trips, Disneyland . . . every day it was something else."

"How was Disneyland?"

"Bruce thought it was great but I think we're getting kind of old for it." I didn't add that Dad had accused me of acting sullen and unpleasant that day or that I had told him it was all his fault. Actually, Dad and I never really talked again after the night we argued over Iris. I kept hoping he'd call me into his room and say, *I've been doing a lot of thinking, Steph . . . and I realize that you and Bruce and Mom are the most important people in my life.* But he didn't. He didn't even say he loves me, that no matter what he'll always love me.

When we got to Alison's the three of us hugged.

"I can't *believe* you and Steph didn't see each other even once!" Rachel said to Alison.

"I know," Alison said. "I was so disappointed but . . . c'est la vie!"

C'est la vie is French for *that's life*.

Gena and Leon came out to greet us and wish us a Happy New Year.

Then we went upstairs to Alison's room. Rachel stretched out on the bed and began to brush Maizie. I sat on the floor with Alison. She pulled a gauzy blue shirt and skirt out of a Christmas box and held it up. "Mom and Leon gave it to me. I'm thinking of wearing it to the dance."

"What dance?" I asked.

"The Ground Hog Day dance," Alison said. "Remember?"

"Oh, that." I had forgotten all about it. "I'll bet none of the seventh grade boys even know how to dance."

"So, we'll teach them!" Alison said.

I thought about teaching Peter Klaff to dance. Would I say, *Forward, to the side, together . . . backward, to the side, together . . .* the way Sadie Wishnik had the day she'd taught Alison and me to rumba in her kitchen?

Maizie turned and grabbed the brush out of Rachel's hand. She jumped off the bed with it between her teeth, carried it across the room and hid it, like a bone, behind Alison's desk.

"You are the silliest dog!" Alison said, scooping her up and kissing her. Maizie wriggled out of Alison's arms and attacked the tissue paper on the floor.

Rachel kind of rolled off the bed, sat behind Alison on the floor and said, "Can I braid your hair?"

"Sure," Alison said.

Last year, when I had long hair, Rachel liked to braid mine.

I made a ball out of tissue paper and tossed it across the room. Maizie chased it.

"Show Alison the bracelet your mother brought you from Venice," Rachel said, as she divided Alison's hair into sections.

"I love Venice!" Alison said. "Muscle Beach . . . the crazies on roller skates . . ."

"Not Venice, California," Rachel said. "Venice, Italy."

"Oh, she went to *that* Venice," Alison said. "Mom and Pierre took me there when I was little. We rode in a gondola."

"This is what she brought me," I said, holding my wrist in front of Alison's face.

"It's beautiful," Alison said.

"Thanks." I made another tissue paper ball and called, "Go get it, Maizie . . ." Then I said, "It was a business trip. Mom had to check out the hotels and restaurants for her clients." I glanced over at Rachel, who was fastening Alison's braids with the barrettes I'd given to her for Christmas.

Alison held her braids out to the sides like Pippi Longstocking, making us laugh. "Want to play Spit?" she asked.

"Sure," I said. Alison has figured out a way for the three of us to play at the same time, by using two decks of cards.

She grabbed them off her desk and handed them to me. I shuffled them and handed them back to her, to cut. Then she handed them to Rachel, to deal.

"When are the two of you going to grow up and quit playing this ridiculous game?" Rachel asked. I couldn't tell if she was serious or joking around.

"Probably never!" Alison said, taking it as a joke.

Rachel began to deal our hands but before we got going Alison said, "If you could dance with only one boy at the Ground Hog Day dance who would it be?"

"I can't think of any boy in seventh grade," Rachel said.

"Suppose it could be any boy at school?" Alison asked.

"Ummm . . ." Rachel said, sticking her tongue into her cheek, "I guess it would be Jeremy Dragon."

"He's in love with Dana," I reminded her.

Rachel put down the cards. "We're not talking about reality," she said. "We're talking about fantasy."

"Even so," I said, "that's a dumb fantasy because you know it can't happen."

"There's no such thing as a dumb fantasy," Rachel said. "Besides, every girl needs a fantasy boyfriend. Isn't that why you have that stupid poster over your bed?"

"But if I had to choose one boy to dance with at the Ground Hog Day dance I wouldn't choose Benjamin Moore. I would know that Benjamin Moore isn't going to be there!"

Rachel shook her head at me. Her eyes had turned very dark. "I have never . . . ever . . . seen anyone act so pre-menstrual in my life! Even Jessica doesn't get as tense as you."

"You know," Alison said, looking me up and down, "I think Rachel might be right this time. You look really puffy and my mother says that's a sure sign."

I didn't tell Alison that the reason I look puffy is that I've gained weight. And I didn't tell Rachel that if I'm acting tense it's for reasons that have nothing to do with getting my period.

"You better start carrying your equipment around with you . . ." Rachel said, "just in case."

"Imagine getting it at school!" Alison said. "What would you do? Where would you go?"

"I'd go to the nurse," I said. "And she'd give me a pad."

"Stephanie doesn't worry about things like that," Rachel said.

"Why should I?" I asked. "Worrying is just a waste of time!"

When I got home I found Mom at the kitchen table folding laundry. Bruce and I had come back from L.A. with our suitcases full of dirty clothes. We hadn't washed anything while we were with Dad. I sat down at the table and Mom pushed the basket of clean clothes toward me. "Rachel says I'm acting pre-menstrual," I told her, as I folded a T-shirt.

Mom hooted. "Sometimes Rachel is just too much!"

"You can say that again!"

"Did you tell her I went to Venice?"

"No."

"Have you told her about Dad and me?"

"No . . . there's nothing to tell."

28

Max Wilson

"Want to see what Jeremy gave me for Christmas?" Dana asked at the bus stop on Monday morning. It was freezing, with snow expected, and we were stomping our feet, trying to keep warm.

I'd never seen Dana look prettier. She was wearing a fuzzy white hat and her cheeks were rosy from the cold. She held out her arm and shook her wrist. "It's his I.D. bracelet. See . . . there's his name."

The bracelet was too big for Dana so she had threaded a small chain through the links. I ran my finger over the letters spelling out *Jeremy Kravitz.* "It's really nice," I said.

"What'd you give him?" Alison asked.

"I gave him my favorite pin. It's a small gold dove. He wears it on his . . ." Dana blushed, then paused as she looked around, but there was no one else listening. "He wears it on his underpants," she whispered, "but nobody knows so don't say anything, okay?"

"Don't worry," I told her. "The three of us know how to keep a secret."

The bus came along then and as soon as we were seated Rachel said, "How does she know?"

"Know what?" I asked.

"Know that he actually wears that pin on his underpants?"

"I see what you mean," I said.

Alison, who was sitting in the row in front of us started to giggle.

"And does he wear it pinned to his waist or his butt?" I asked.

"Or someplace else?" Rachel said.

"Oh, no . . ." Alison said, "that's too disgusting!"

"Besides," I said, "wouldn't that hurt?"

By the time Jeremy Dragon got on the bus we were laughing so hard we just about fell off our seats as he passed us. "What's so funny, Macbeth?" he asked. Sometimes he calls the three of us Macbeth as if we are just one person. He didn't wait for us to answer, not that we would have been able to, anyway. He walked to the middle of the bus where Dana was saving a seat for him.

When Alison and I got to homeroom we found a substitute teacher at Mrs. Remo's desk. She was cleaning her glasses, a routine she repeated about twenty times before the last bell rang. Then she stood and introduced herself. "Good morning, class," she said, in a high-pitched voice. "I'm Mrs. Zeller. This is my first day as a substitute teacher."

Admitting that was a real mistake! Notes started flying across the room.

"I used to teach," Mrs. Zeller continued, "before my children were born, but I taught in high school, not junior high."

That did it. Everyone began to laugh out loud.

Mrs. Zeller looked around, trying to figure out the joke. She didn't know she was it. "I taught in Ohio," she said, "not Connecticut."

Now we were roaring, as if that was the funniest line in the history of the world.

Mrs. Zeller fiddled with the blue beads around her neck, tucked a loose strand of hair back into place, then tugged at her skirt and looked down. She probably thought she was losing her underwear.

"Well . . ." she said, "I guess I have to tell you

the bad news. Mrs. Remo's father passed away over the holidays so she's going to be out all week."

A hush fell over the room. I never even knew Mrs. Remo had a father. I hardly ever think of my teachers as regular people with families and lives outside of school. I wonder if they ever think of us that way. I wonder if they know that sometimes kids can't concentrate in class because of what's going on at home. I'm lucky that I can put my family problems out of my mind while I'm at school. I looked over at Alison. She was clutching her favorite stone. I thought back to that day right after Thanksgiving when Mrs. Remo had shouted at Alison and me, then kept us after school. Rachel had said, *Maybe Mrs. Remo didn't have a good Thanksgiving*. Rachel could have been right.

Amber Ackbourne, who had been laughing harder than anyone before Mrs. Zeller told us the bad news, was crying now. Her shoulders shook and she sounded like a sick cat. I thought how weird it is that one minute you can be having the greatest time and the next . . . *wham* . . . just like that everything changes.

The door to our homeroom opened and a tall boy walked over to Mrs. Zeller. He handed her a yellow card and said, "I'm Max Wilson. I'm new."

Amber Ackbourne blew her nose and pulled herself together.

"Oh, dear," Mrs. Zeller said, her hands fluttering around her blue beads. "A new boy. What do we do about new people, class?"

Eric Macaulay called, "Give him a desk."

"Yes," Mrs. Zeller said, "of course. A desk. That would be a good place to start. Why don't you find a desk, Max, and make yourself at home. I'm a substitute and this is my first day, so I don't know the ropes yet." She sounded less nervous than before.

Max walked around the room looking for a desk. When he didn't find one he said, "Excuse me, but there's no desk."

"No desk," Mrs. Zeller said. "What now?"

"Give him a chair," Eric Macaulay said. "Then you can ask the janitor to bring up another desk. A big desk because this guy is tall."

"Thank you," Mrs. Zeller said. "That's very good advice. What did you say your name was?"

"Eric Macaulay."

"Well, thank you, Eric, for being so helpful," Mrs. Zeller said.

Max found a chair and sat down.

"Now, Max . . ." Mrs. Zeller said, "why don't you tell us something about yourself . . . something to help us get acquainted with you."

"There's nothing to tell," Max said.

"There must be something," Mrs. Zeller said. "Tell us where you came from and about your family."

Max sat low in his chair, his legs stretched straight out in front of him. He was wearing black hi-tops. "I'm from Kansas City," he said, looking into his lap. "That's in Missouri. There is a Kansas City in Kansas but that's not the big one. My father got transferred up here so that's how come we moved. I've got two sisters and a brother. My brother's older than me and my sisters are younger. That's about it." His voice cracked on every other word. "Oh yeah . . ." he added and this time he looked up. "I was thirteen on New Year's day and I like basketball." He smiled. He looked good when he smiled.

He had short brown hair, hazel eyes and a nose that was too big for his face. Mom says people have to grow into their noses. She says sometimes it takes until you're thirty. That's a long time to wait for your face to catch up with your nose.

"That was very interesting, Max," Mrs. Zeller said.

Eric Macaulay waved his hand and called, "Mrs. Zeller . . . how about if I introduce the rest of the class to Max?"

"What a good idea, Eric," Mrs. Zeller said.

I loved the way Eric was doing his Remarkable

Eyes number on Mrs. Zeller. He walked up and down the rows of desks saying our names, then giving each of us a title. Peter Klaff was Mr. Shy, Amber Ackbourne was the National Enquirer and Alison was Miss Popularity. When he came to me he rested his hand on my head. I squirmed, trying to move away from him. "And this is Stephanie Hirsch," he said, "also known as Hershey Bar, also known as El Chunko."

El Chunko! I didn't wait for another word. I shoved my chair back and stood up so fast it toppled over. "And this . . . in case you're wondering . . ." I said, pointing at Eric, "this is the Class Asshole!"

Everyone laughed like crazy for a minute, then the room fell silent again. Mrs. Zeller looked right at me and said, "I'm going to forget I heard you use that word in class . . . but I never want to hear it again. Do you understand?"

I wiped my sweaty palms off on my jeans. "Yes," I said.

Then the bell rang and everybody rushed off to their first period classes.

At lunchtime the first one of us to reach the cafeteria gets on line and buys three cartons of milk. Today it was me. But Alison met me at the cash register. "Eric didn't mean anything, you know," she said. "It was just his idea of a joke."

"Some joke!" I walked across the cafeteria in a huff.

Alison followed. "Please don't be mad at me."

"I'm not mad at you. I just don't see how you can like him."

"Mom says there's no accounting for taste," Alison said.

"I guess this proves she's right!"

The three of us share a lunch table with Miri Levine, Kara Klaff and two other girls. Eric Macaulay, Peter Klaff and their friends sit two tables away from us. Today they also had Max Wilson with them. I set the milk cartons down and took a seat with my back to the boys. Rachel sat opposite me. "Who is that guy?" she asked.

"What guy?" I said.

"That comely guy with Eric and Peter."

"What's comely?" Alison asked.

"Attractive . . . good looking . . . cute . . ."

"You think he's cute?" I said.

"Yes," Rachel said, "very."

"Then why didn't you just say so in the first place?" I asked.

"Because I like the way comely sounds," Rachel said. "I think it suits him."

"His name is Max Wilson," Alison told her. "He's new . . . he's in our homeroom . . . he's from Kansas City."

"The one in Missouri," I added, as I opened my lunch bag and spread out a tunafish sandwich with lettuce, tomato and mayonnaise, a bag of Fritos, two doughnuts and an apple.

"He's in my Spanish class," Alison continued, "and he couldn't answer one question. He's a complete airhead."

"I'll bet he's at least 5'8"," Rachel said, staring.

"Did you hear what Alison said?" I asked. "She *said* he's a complete airhead."

"You can't judge a person's intelligence by how he behaves in one class on his first day at a new school," Rachel said.

"Especially if he's a *comely* new person," Alison said.

"Oh, right," I added, "especially if he's *really* comely." Alison and I laughed and laughed.

Rachel pushed up her sleeves. "Sometimes the two of *you* act like complete airheads!"

29

El Chunko

Aunt Denise gave Mom an exercise tape for Christmas. When Mom got home from work on Monday night, she put on shorts and a T-shirt, shoved the tape into the VCR and jumped around doing something called Jazzercise.

I made myself a snack of rye bread slathered with cream cheese, then curled up in my favorite chair in the den and watched as Mom huffed and puffed her way through the tape. Mom is shaped like a pear, small on top and wider on the bottom. She says there's nothing you can do about the way you're built. It's all in the genes.

I draped my legs over the arm of the chair and devoured the rye bread as Mom lay on her mat doing some kind of fancy sit-ups to an old Michael Jackson song. Mom copied everything the Jazzercise leader did. When the leader asked, *Are you smiling?* Mom smiled. When she asked, *Are you still breathing?* Mom shouted, "Yes!"

"You know what Eric Macaulay called me today?" I asked Mom.

"What?" she said, without missing a beat.

"He called me El Chunko . . . so then I called him an asshole."

I expected Mom to give me a lecture about using unacceptable language at school. But instead she said, "You have gained weight, Steph. Why don't you join me . . . Jazzercise is fun!" She was on her hands and knees raising one leg to the side, then the other. Each time she did, she groaned.

"It doesn't look like fun," I said.

"It's not as bad as it looks." She was panting so hard she could barely talk.

When that number was over the Jazzercise leader applauded and said, *Give your gluts a hand!*

Mom sat up and applauded, too.

"Where are your gluts?" I asked.

"Back here," Mom said, grabbing the lower part of her backside.

"Oh," I said.

The next day Mom brought home a scale. When she stepped on it her weight across the screen in red numbers. "You're ne. Steph."

"No thanks."

"Come on . . ."

"I *said* no thanks!"

"Look," Mom said, "I know you don't want to talk about this but I'm concerned about your health. I need to know exactly how much weight you've gained since the school year began."

"A few pounds," I said. Actually, I had no idea how much weight I'd gained. The school nurse weighs us the first week of school but other than that I haven't been near a scale.

"Stephanie," Mom said, sounding very serious, "get on the scale."

"Not with my clothes on."

"Okay . . . then get undressed."

"Not in front of you."

"I'm your mother."

"I know! That's the point."

"Then get undressed in the bathroom . . . but hurry up."

I could tell Mom was losing patience with me. So I went to the bathroom, took off all my clothes, wrapped myself in a towel, then ran back to Mom's room and stepped on the scale.

"Stephanie!" Mom said, as the numbers flashed.

least ten pounds overweight,"

...t's exactly right. I'm calling Dr. ...rning. We've got to do something

"Do... Dr. Klaff!" I said. I could just see the Klaff family at the dinner table talking about me. *Stephanie Hirsch has gained quite a bit of weight,* Dr. Klaff would say.

And Kara would say, *I'm not surprised. I'm at her lunch table and she's been pigging out since Thanksgiving.*

Then Peter would say, *I used to like her, but that was before she turned into El Chunko. Now I'm not so sure. I don't even know if I'm going to dance with her at the Ground Hog Day dance.*

Then Kara would say, *But Peter . . . if you don't, who will?*

"I want Dr. Klaff to recommend a sensible diet," Mom was saying, "not one of those fad diets that ruins your health."

"Who said anything about a diet?" I asked.

"How do you expect to lose weight without a diet and exercise?"

"I don't know."

That night after dinner Mom cleaned out the pantry. She got rid of every cookie, pretzel and potato chip. Then she attacked the freezer, pulling out the frozen cakes and doughnuts. "From now on," she said, "it's carrot and celery sticks for snacks."

I watched as Mom packed all the goodies into a shopping bag. "What are you going to do with them?"

"I'm taking them to Aunt Denise's house. Howard and his friends can have it all."

"Don't you care about his weight and health?"

"Howard is as thin as a flagpole," Mom said.

"I'm going to starve," I said. "I won't have enough energy left to exercise."

"You'll have more energy than you do now," Mom told me. "Wait and see."

That night I stood naked in front of the full length mirror on the back of the bathroom door. It was steamy from my bath, but I could see enough. My breasts were growing or else they were just fat. It was hard to tell. Maybe if I lost weight, I'd lose them, too. My gluts were pretty disgusting. When I jumped up and down they shook. The hair down there, my pubic hair, was growing thicker. It was much darker than the hair on my head. My legs weren't bad but my feet were funny-looking. My second toes were longer than my big toes.

"Stephanie!" Bruce called, banging on the bathroom door. "I've got to go."

I put on my robe and opened the door. "It's all yours."

"I can't breathe in here," he said, fanning the air. "Why do you have to steam it up every night?"

"Steam is good for you," I told him. "It opens your pores."

"Where are your pores?"

"You'll find out when you're my age."

30

Flings

The phone rang just as we were finishing dinner the next night. It was Dad.

"How's school?" he asked me.

"Fine."

"How are Rachel and Alison?"

"Fine."

"How's the weather?"

"Cold with a chance of snow."

"What's new?"

"Nothing."

After that there was a minute of silence. Probably Dad was trying to think of some other question for me. When he couldn't he said, "Well . . . why don't you put Bruce on?"

I was at my desk later, doing math homework

and humming along with the Top Forty songs on my radio, when Mom came to my room. She stood behind me with her hands resting lightly on my shoulders. "Did something happen between you and Dad over the holidays?" When I didn't answer Mom continued, "I couldn't help noticing how distant you were to him on the phone."

"It has to do with Iris," I said. This was the first time I'd said Iris's name at home.

"Is she the woman Dad's seeing?"

"Yes. I wasn't sure if you knew."

"I don't know the details," Mom said, "but I know he's met someone."

"Doesn't it bother you?" I asked.

"I guess I don't like the idea of being replaced so easily."

I turned around and faced Mom. "You're not being replaced! Iris is just a fling."

Mom laughed.

"It's not funny!"

"I know . . . and you're probably right . . . it's just a fling."

I was glad Mom agreed with me. I felt a lot better until she said, "I imagine I'll have my own fling one of these days."

"You!" I said. "When?"

"I don't know."

"Will it be before or after my birthday?"

Mom laughed again.

"I'm serious," I told her. "I want to know."

"Forget it, Steph."

"No, I'm not going to forget it. Is having a fling part of a trial separation? Is it something everyone does?"

"I was just kidding," Mom said.

But I knew she wasn't.

31

Thoughts

Jeremy Dragon is available again! But the three of us can't be happy about it because Dana is so miserable. She came to the bus stop the following Monday morning with red and swollen eyes. "It's all over," she said, holding up her naked wrist.

"What happened?" Rachel asked.

"We went to a party and he made out with Marcella, that eighth grade slut." Tears spilled down her cheeks.

Alison put her arm around Dana's waist. "I'm really sorry."

I gave Dana a tissue to blow her nose.

"I trusted him," Dana said. "I trusted him with my innermost feelings and he betrayed me."

I felt a lump in my throat. If this was love you could have it!

"I don't know how I'm going to face him on the bus this morning," Dana said. "Do you think I could sit with the three of you . . . because my closest friends don't ride this bus and . . ."

"We'd be honored," Rachel said.

"And we'll never speak to Jeremy again!" I promised.

When the bus stopped we got on and found seats together. At the next stop, when Jeremy got on and greeted us in his usual way, "Hey, Macbeth!" we turned away from him.

I was very glad to see Mrs. Remo back at her desk in homeroom. Mrs. Zeller had never forgiven me for saying the A-word in class, and I'd felt uncomfortable around her all week long. After Mrs. Remo took attendance she stood and said, "I want to thank all of you for your kind thoughts and generous contribution to the Cancer Society in memory of my father. He was a fine man and I'm going to miss him very much." She choked up. "But he had a long, productive life and that's what counts."

I felt another lump in my throat. This one was even bigger than the one at the bus stop. This one made me think about my father. Sometimes I feel guilty because I don't miss him that much, especially since the holidays. I think if he would just stay in L.A. everything would be okay. Maybe it would be different if Mom cried all the time or seemed depressed, but she doesn't. I think it would be a lot harder for us if Dad lived nearby and we had to go visit him and Iris.

Still, as Mrs. Remo told us about her father, I imagined all the terrible things that could happen to Dad. I imagined him crashing into a van on the Freeway, drowning in the ocean, having a heart attack at work. I couldn't stand the idea of anything happening to him, especially if he didn't know I still love him.

As soon as I got to math class I opened my notebook and started a letter.

Dear Dad,

I was thinking of you this morning. And I was wondering if you think I don't love you anymore? In case you don't know, I still do. But sometimes I get really mad and I don't know how to tell you. I got really mad about you and Iris because Bruce and I thought we were coming to L.A. to spend the holidays just with you. So naturally we were surprised and disappointed to find Iris there. Also, I hate it when you ask me so many questions over the phone. I especially hate it when you ask me about the weather. You never ask Bruce about the weather. If you want to know about the weather that much why don't you listen to the national weather report? Another thing is, I was wondering how you feel about me . . .

Alison tugged at my arm. "Steph . . . he just called you to the board."

I looked up and Mr. Burns was staring at me. "I won't even ask where your mind is this morning, Stephanie. It's clear that it's somewhere else. But if you wouldn't mind taking your turn at the board . . ."

I walked up to the blackboard and stood between Peter Klaff and Emily Giordano. Somehow I was able to solve the problem quickly and get it right. I would have to finish my letter to Dad during English.

But once a week, when we come into Mr. Diamond's class, we have a special writing assignment. And today was the day. Mr. Diamond had printed the topic on the board: *I Used To Be . . . But I'm Not Anymore.* Mr. Diamond never grades these papers. He just writes comments. Also, spelling and grammar don't count. What counts is our ideas and how we present them. The following week he'll choose two or three papers to read out loud but he never tells us who wrote them. Sometimes you can figure it out, though.

He always picks the best papers to read, papers that make you think.

I sat for a long time before I started to write. I looked up at the ceiling for inspiration, then out the window, but all I saw were the tops of bare trees. I nibbled on my pencil. *I Used To Be . . . But I'm Not Anymore*. I looked around the classroom. Almost everyone else was hard at work.

I thought about the letter I'd started to Dad during math class. I thought about how my life has changed. And then an idea came to me and I began to write. I wrote and wrote, filling up one sheet of paper after another. When the bell rang I looked up at the clock and couldn't believe the time had gone so quickly. I clipped my five pages together and wrote across the bottom: *Please do not read this aloud in class.*

At lunchtime Rachel begged me to introduce her to Max. "Please, Steph . . . I have to meet him!"

"Okay . . . okay . . ." I said. The two of us got on line right behind him. "Hey, Max!" I said, tapping him on the back. "How're you doing?"

He looked at me.

"Stephanie," I said. "From your homeroom . . ."

"Oh, yeah . . ." he said. "You're El Chunko, right?"

I gritted my teeth. "You can call me either Stephanie or Steph, but that's it!"

"Sure," Max said. "It's nothing to me . . . you know? I'll call you whatever you want."

Rachel gave me a little kick, reminding me to introduce her to him.

"Oh, Max," I said, "I'd like you to meet my friend, Rachel Robinson. She's in 7-202 . . . that's the homeroom right next to ours."

"You're in seventh grade?" Max asked Rachel.

"Yes," Rachel said.

"You're tall for seventh grade," Max said.

"So are you," Rachel told him.

Max laughed. He sounded like a horse.

"So . . ." Rachel said, "everything's up to date in Kansas City . . . right?"

"Huh?" Max said.

"Never mind," Rachel said. "It's just a song."

"You know a song about Kansas City?" Max asked.

"Yes . . . it's from a musical called *Oklahoma!*"

"Whoa . . ." Max said, "this is going too fast for me."

We reached the food counter and Max took fish cakes, mashed potatoes and peas. Nothing makes the cafeteria smell as bad as fish cakes.

Max put mustard on his. "Aren't you getting anything?" he asked us.

"We bring our lunch," I told him. "But we buy our milk."

Max followed us to our table. "Mind if I join you?"

"Uh . . . all the seats at this table are taken," Rachel said. "Why don't you sit with Eric and Peter?"

"They're not as pretty as you," Max said to Rachel.

Rachel turned purple and took a deep breath.

Max leaned over and spoke softly. "Some day I'd like to hear that song about Kansas City."

As soon as he was gone Rachel said, "I've got to get something new to wear to the Ground Hog Day dance."

"He seems to like you fine just the way you are," I told her.

"He did seem to like me, didn't he?"

"Yes."

"You think he really does or was it just an act?"

"I don't think it was an act."

"Suppose he really *does* like me?"

"So . . . you want him to, don't you?"

"I think I do but . . ." Rachel watched me as I unpacked my lunch. "A hardboiled egg and carrot sticks?" she asked.

"Mom and I are watching our weight."

"Is it because the boys are calling you El Chunko?"

"It has nothing to do with them!"

32

The Celebrity

Bruce won second place in the *Kids for Peace* poster contest. The reporters who came to our house to interview him had questions for me, too. "Tell us, Stephanie . . . how does it feel to have a brother who's so involved in the peace movement?"

"I'm very proud of my little brother," I told them. I kept stressing *little* and *younger* when I talked about Bruce. And I didn't say one word about his nightmares.

"Your brother seems to have a very supportive family. Would you say that's true?"

"Oh, yes . . . definitely."

"Have your parents encouraged him in his quest for peace?"

"Let's put it this way," I told them. "They haven't discouraged him."

"Then they're not activists themselves?"

"Pardon?" That's the word Rachel uses when she's talking to grownups and she doesn't get what they mean.

Mom had been standing across the living room with Bruce, who was being interviewed by another reporter. Now she walked over to me and put her arm around my shoulder.

"Mrs. Hirsch . . ." the reporter said, "I was just asking Stephanie if you or Mr. Hirsch are activists in the peace movement?"

"Well, no . . ." Mom said, "not exactly . . . although we certainly believe in it. My business takes up most of my time."

"And your husband?"

"He's in California . . . also on business."

"So what you're saying is that your ten-year-old son did this on his own?"

"Yes, that's right."

War Is Stupid! Says Ten-Year-Old Poster Winner, the headline read in the Sunday paper. Under that was a picture of Bruce and a story about him.

Bruce called Dad to tell him the good news. And Dad called Bruce two more times over the weekend. The first time I answered the phone. He said, "Isn't it great about your brother!"

And I said, "Yes."

"I'll bet the phone hasn't stopped ringing."

"Mom's thinking of taking it off the hook."

"Wish I were there to celebrate with you."

I didn't respond.

"Well, let me talk to Bruce."

After he called *again* I asked Bruce, "What'd he want this time?"

Bruce said, "You know . . . more about being proud of me. And he wanted to remind me to wear a tie and jacket to the White House."

On Monday, at the bus stop, Dana said, "I saw Bruce's picture in the paper yesterday. He's so famous!"

"Yeah . . . he is," I said.

"Did he leave for Washington yet?" Rachel asked.

"He's leaving at nine," I told her. Mom is going with him. Bruce and the other poster winners are meeting the President this afternoon. Then they're flying to New York and staying overnight at a hotel because tomorrow morning they're going to be on the *Today* show. I'm going to spend the night at Aunt Denise's.

"Have you heard about me and Jeremy?" Dana asked.

"No . . . what?" I asked.

She shook her wrist. She was wearing Jeremy's I.D. bracelet again.

"What happened?" Rachel asked.

"He realized he'd made a terrible mistake and he begged me to forgive him."

"That's so romantic," Alison said.

"I wouldn't have forgiven him that easily," Rachel said.

"Just wait until you're in love!" Dana said.

Rachel didn't tell her that she's halfway there.

At school everybody was talking about Bruce, including my teachers. Mrs. Remo said, "What a special brother you must have, Stephanie."

By the end of the day I was sick of hearing about Bruce and how great he is. So when Mr. Diamond called me up to his desk after class I figured it was going to be more of the same. "Stephanie . . . that paper was amazing!"

"It wasn't that great," I told him, thinking he meant the story in the newspaper.

"Believe me," he said, "it was very special."

It wasn't until he tapped the paper he was holding that I realized he wasn't talking about the newspaper. He was talking about the paper I'd written in class last week. Across the top in green ink he had printed, *Interesting, revealing and straight from the heart!*

"I've asked Mrs. Balaban to see you this afternoon," Mr. Diamond said.

"Who's Mrs. Balaban?"

"The school counselor. She might be able to help you sort out your problems."

"I don't have any problems."

"I know these things are hard to face, Stephanie . . ."

"What things?"

"The kinds of problems you wrote about."

"No," I said, "you've got it all wrong!"

"Stephanie . . ." Mr. Diamond said, "go and see Mrs. Balaban."

"Sit down, Stephanie," Mrs. Balaban said.

I sat in the chair at the side of her desk. She was wearing a white sweater with a design knitted into it. On one hand her fingernails were long and polished pink. But on the other, three of her nails were very short and not polished at all. There was a picture of a baby on her desk.

When she caught me looking at it she turned it toward me and said, "This is Hilary . . . she's a year old now but she was only eight months when this was taken."

"She's cute."

Mrs. Balaban smiled and flicked her long, dark hair out of her way. "Do you have brothers or sisters?"

"I have one brother. He's ten. You probably read about him in yesterday's paper. He won second place in the *Kids for Peace* poster contest. He's going to meet the President and be on the *Today* show."

"Really . . ." Mrs. Balaban said. "And how do you feel about that?"

"Me? Well . . . I'm glad for Bruce but I wouldn't mind being famous myself." I laughed. It didn't sound like my regular laugh.

Mrs. Balaban lowered her voice as if she were telling me a secret. "Everything said in this office is strictly confidential, Stephanie."

"Good," I said.

Then we just looked at each other for the longest time. It reminded me of the staring contests we'd had at Girl Scout camp, where whoever blinks first, loses. Mrs. Balaban blinked first. "In February I'm starting an after school group for kids whose parents have split up."

"My parents haven't split up."

"Oh?" Mrs. Balaban studied the hand with the long fingernails. "Well, Stephanie . . . we can talk about anything that's on your mind . . . anything that's bothering you."

"Nothing's bothering me."

"I see." She sharpened two yellow pencils. Then she said, "If you ever do want to talk I'll be here. I'm on your side. I hope you'll remember that."

"Okay."

"Thanks for stopping by." She reached across her desk and shook my hand. "I'm trying to meet as many new students as I can."

"There's a new boy in my homeroom," I said. "Max Wilson. He's very tall. Maybe you should meet him."

"Max Wilson . . ." Mrs. Balaban repeated, writing it down.

On Tuesday morning Aunt Denise and I watched the *Today* show together. Bruce came on right after the eight o'clock news. Aunt Denise grabbed my arm and held on during the entire interview, which lasted five minutes. Bruce looked like he was having a good time. The other two poster winners seemed scared. I was glad when the interview was over because Aunt Denise stopped crying and finally let go of my arm.

I decided I'd send Dad the paper I wrote in Mr. Diamond's class.

I Used To Be An Optimist But I'm Not Anymore

It's not as easy to be an optimist now that I'm almost thirteen because I know a lot more than I used to . . .

Dad is always asking how I'm doing in school. This would prove that some of my work is *interesting, revealing and straight from the heart.*

33

Making Plans

Mom bought new earrings. They're shaped like bolts of lightning and they sparkle. "What do you think?" she asked. The earrings dangled from her ear lobes to her chin.

"They're different," I said.

"I hope that's a compliment."

I didn't want to hurt Mom's feelings so I didn't tell her the earrings were much too flashy. "Are you going to wear them to the office?"

"No," Mom said, "I'm going to wear them to Carla's party on Saturday night."

"I didn't know Carla's having a party."

"Yes," Mom said, "and I told her I'd come in for the weekend to give her a hand."

"Who's coming to this party?" I asked.

"Carla's friends."

"Women *and* men?"

"Yes," Mom said, "of course."

"Married *and* divorced?"

"I really don't know. I imagine there will be some of each."

"And you're going to wear *those* earrings?"

"Yes," Mom said, "but I'm also going to wear a dress and shoes and . . ."

"This is it, isn't it?" I asked.

"This is what?"

"You're going to New York to have your fling."

Mom threw back her head and laughed. The earrings danced around her face.

"It's not funny!" I said. I hate it when I'm being serious and Mom thinks it's a big joke.

But Mom couldn't stop laughing. Finally, she managed to say, "Sorry . . . it just struck me as funny that you should be worried about me having a fling." She gulped, holding back another laugh.

"I'm not worried!" I told her. "I never worry! I just don't like the idea of you with some guy. I'll probably hate him as much as I hate Iris."

"I didn't know you hate Iris," Mom said, quietly.

"Well, now you know. It may be fun for you and Dad to have your flings but it's not fun for Bruce and me."

"I'm sorry, Steph . . . I keep forgetting this is hard on you."

"People who are separated are supposed to be miserable," I told her.

"On some days I am," Mom said, "but I try to keep busy and not give in to it."

I thought about how I do the same thing.

"Look . . ." Mom said, "I need to get out and be with people. That's all there is to it." She took off her new earrings and dropped them into her jewelry box. "So would you rather spend the weekend at Aunt Denise's or with a friend?"

"With a friend," I said.

As I was getting ready for bed I decided I'd ask Alison if I could spend the weekend at her house.

"It's all set," Mom said, when she came to my room to say goodnight. "Nell Robinson would love to have you for the weekend."

"But Mom . . . I was going to ask Alison."

Mom shook her head. "I assumed when you said you wanted to stay with a friend you meant Rachel."

"You should have asked me first," I told her.

"I can see that now," Mom said, rescuing Wiley Coyote from the floor. She set him on my chair. "You don't mind going to Rachel's, do you?"

"It's not that I mind . . ."

"Good . . ." Mom said, before I'd finished. "Because it would be awkward to try to explain to Nell now. Besides, I'll feel more comfortable knowing you're at the Robinsons'."

"I keep telling you that Gena Farrell is just a regular person," I said. "You don't have to be afraid of her."

"I'm not the least bit afraid of her," Mom said. "It's just that I've known Nell longer."

I happen to know that Mom thinks of Gena Farrell as a famous TV star, not as Alison's mother. One time, when Gena came by our house to pick up Alison, Mom talked too fast and offered Gena a cup of tea at least ten times, until finally Gena said, "Thanks . . . I'd love a cup." Alison says that just because Gena is famous and beautiful people don't treat her the same as they would somebody else. And that makes *her* feel uncomfortable.

Bruce understands. He told me he's sick of being famous. The other night he said, "It was fun for a few days but I never want to see another reporter. I hate their dumb questions. And I'm never entering another contest. From now on I just want to be a regular kid and play with David after school."

"But if you had it to do over again, would you still enter this contest?" I asked.

"Maybe," Bruce said. "Because it wasn't that bad meeting the President and having cocoa at the White House."

At the bus stop the next morning Rachel said, "I hear you're coming for the weekend."

"Yes," I told her. "Mom is going to New York to help her friend give a party."

"So what do you want to do?" Rachel asked.

"I don't know . . . whatever you want to do."

"I was planning on rehearsing a new piece with Stacey Green but I can cancel," Rachel said.

"You don't have to cancel," I told her. "I can do something else while you're rehearsing."

"Really . . . you wouldn't mind?" Rachel asked.

"No . . . when are you going to rehearse?"

"Friday night."

"We can go to the movies," Alison said to me. "And you can sleep over at my house."

"No," Rachel said. "My mother's looking forward to having Steph stay at our house."

Her *mother* is looking forward to having me stay? I thought. I guess that proved Mrs. Robinson hadn't discussed Rachel's weekend plans with her, either.

"And don't forget . . ." Alison said, "on Saturday we're going shopping for the Ground Hog Day dance."

"I won't forget," Rachel said, "I'm going to get something really wild!"

"What do you mean by wild?" I asked.

"You know," Rachel said. "Wild!"

Like Mom's earrings, I thought.

34

Getting Even

Dad called. "I got your letter and essay, Steph."

"Just forget about it," I told him.

"I don't want to forget about it," Dad said. "It took me a while to digest everything you said but now I think I understand."

"There's nothing to understand. I was in a weird mood that day . . . that's all."

"No . . . it was foolish of me to expect you and Bruce to accept Iris on such short notice," Dad said.

"You mean on *no* notice."

I could hear Dad sigh. "I should have told you about her before you came."

"It doesn't matter," I said. "I understand now that you and Mom have to have your flings."

"What do you mean?"

"Nothing . . . just that after this weekend you and Mom will be even."

"What are you talking about?" Dad said. "What's this about Rowena having a fling?"

I could tell from the change in his voice that he didn't like the idea at all. So I added, "You should see the earrings she got for Carla's party. They're really wild!"

"Put Mom on the phone," Dad said.

"She's not here."

"Where is she?"

"She drove Bruce over to Aunt Denise's. Uncle Richard's taking him and Howard to a hockey game."

"Ask her to call as soon as she gets back," Dad said.

"She might be too busy packing for the weekend," I told him.

"Well . . . tell her I called."

"Okay."

"And Steph . . ." Dad said, "about your birthday . . ."

I was glad to hear he remembered.

"I'm thinking of flying in for the weekend."

No! I thought. I don't want him flying in for the weekend. Look how excited I had been about Thanksgiving and then he came home and spoiled everything with his news about the separation. I don't want any bad news over my birthday weekend! So I said, "I'm going to be really busy. We're having a dance at school on Friday night and on Saturday Gran Lola and Papa Jack are taking Rachel, Alison and me to a play. And on Sunday Mom's having the family over for cake. She's already ordered it . . . it's going to have purple roses . . ."

"Maybe I should wait until spring break," Dad said.

"That would be better."

"But I'm sending your birthday surprise now."

"What is it?"

"If I tell you it won't be a surprise."

Probably another sweatshirt, I thought.

Sleep-over

On Friday morning at the bus stop Dana held out her arm and the bracelet was gone. "This time it's for good!" she told us.

"What happened?" Alison asked.

"He says he wants to be free to go out with other girls . . . like Marcella."

"Don't worry," Rachel said, "it's probably just sexual attraction."

"Please don't say that!" Dana started to cry.

"All she means is that Jeremy's had a lot of experience," I said, trying to make Dana feel better.

"How do you know that?" Dana stared at me.

"Because he's got . . ." I was going to say "hairy legs" but Rachel kicked me.

tephanie means," Rachel said, "is that boys are so interested in sex they forget about everything else. He'll come to his senses one of these days."

"I don't know," Dana said, blowing her nose. "I'm very confused. My friends tell me he's trying to make me jealous. They say he's trying to pressure me into going further than I want to go."

"You should never allow yourself to be pressured into having sex," Rachel said, sounding like an expert.

"That's right," I added, as if I knew all about it, too.

"Absolutely," Alison agreed.

"Your generation is just amazing!" Dana told us. "When I was your age I didn't know anything."

That night at the movie theater I bought a small container of popcorn. So did Alison but she got hers with butter and I didn't. As soon as we sat down I found out that popcorn without butter is very dry. It sticks in your throat. I started choking on the first piece I ate. So I excused myself to go back to the lobby for a drink of water. The people in our row had to stand to let me out. After I got a drink I stood on the refreshment line again, this time to have my popcorn buttered. It's probably not real butter anyway, I told myself, remembering my promise to Mom—that I'd watch what I ate over the weekend. It's probably just something to wet down the popcorn so you can eat it without choking to death.

While I was waiting Jeremy Dragon came into the theater with Marcella. She was wearing the tightest jeans I'd ever seen, tucked into white cowboy boots. And she was chewing bubble gum. I hoped she'd blow a bubble big enough to get stuck in her eye makeup.

By the time my popcorn was buttered the lights had gone down inside the theater and I had trouble spotting Alison. But I didn't have any trouble spotting Jeremy and Marcella. They were sitting in the last row, over on the side, and they were already making out. I wondered what Marcella had done with her bubble gum? Or did she kiss with it still in her mouth? No, she was the type who'd stick it under her seat.

By the time I found Alison the movie had begun. Everyone in our row had to stand so I could pass. As soon as I was seated I told Alison about Jeremy and Marcella. The woman behind us tapped me on the shoulder and said, "Shush . . ."

Right after the opening scene Alison whispered, "I'm going out for a drink."

I nodded. Everyone had to stand again, as Alison made her way to the end of our row.

She was gone for at least ten minutes and when she came back the man on her other side said, "Will you girls either quit running around or find yourselves some other seats!" So the two of us got up and went to look for other seats.

We stood at the back of the theater for a while, watching Jeremy and Marcella, until the usher told us that we either had to find seats or leave the theater. The only seats we could find were in the first row. We were so close to the screen we had to strain our necks to see. The movie wasn't worth it.

After, we went to the frozen yogurt place, where Leon was going to pick us up at ten. I ordered a cup of pineapple yogurt. That's about as simple as you get. Alison had her favorite— a PeachBerry Smoothie. As we were waiting for our orders Jeremy and Marcella came in. "Hey, Macbeth . . ." Jeremy called, "enjoy the show?"

I was really surprised. First of all I didn't know he'd seen us in the theater. Second of all I didn't know which show he meant—the movie or the show he and Marcella had put on. So I just looked at him and said, "I've seen better."

He laughed. "I'll bet."

Marcella ordered a waffle cone with pecan praline yogurt. She didn't speak to either one of us.

When Leon pulled up, twenty minutes later, he asked Alison to run back inside to buy a quart of pistachio to go. "Gena's got a craving for pistachio," he told me, as I got into the back seat of the car.

Rachel was sitting up in bed, reading, when I got to her house. Her face was covered with some kind of white goo.

"What is that?" I asked.

"It's a mask," Rachel said. "It dries up your skin so you won't break out."

"You sleep with it?"

"No, you wash it off after fifteen minutes. So how was the movie?"

"I've seen better," I told her. "But Jeremy and Marcella were there . . . making out."

"Making out in public is *so* disgusting!" Rachel said.

"I know. It was very embarrassing to have to watch them kiss."

"You actually saw them kiss?"

"Yes, more than once," I told her. "So how was rehearsal with Stacey?"

"Frustrating. We tried a really hard piece," Rachel said. "So how did they kiss?"

"The usual way."

"French?"

"I wasn't *that* close," I said.

"I'll never make out at the movies for the whole town to see," Rachel said.

"Me neither."

"If you feel like reading there's a really good book on my desk."

I walked over to Rachel's desk. "Which one?" I asked. There was a whole stack.

"It's called *Gone With the Wind*," Rachel said. "You'll like it. It's very romantic."

"I'm not into romances the way I was last year," I told her.

"This isn't like some teenage romance," she said. "This is the real thing."

I thumbed through the book. "It's very long."

"But it goes fast once you get into it."

"I think I'll wait a while to try this one."

"Okay," Rachel said, yawning. "I'll wash off my mask . . . then we can go to sleep."

I got undressed while Rachel was in the bathroom. If only we were as close as we used to be, I thought, I would tell her about my parents. I wish I could . . . I wish I could tell her *and* Alison. I hate having to keep secrets from my best friends. I've never kept a secret from Rachel before and until this year she's never kept one from me. But everything is different between us now. I can't explain it but I can feel it.

I pulled my nightgown over my head, then settled into my sleeping bag, which was spread out on a foam pad on the rug. It would be easy to tell Alison about my parents, I thought. She'd understand, especially since she's been through it herself. But I could never tell her without telling Rachel, too.

Rachel came back and got into bed. " 'Night," she said, turning out the light.

"Rachel . . ."

"Yeah?"

"Remember when we used to play dress-up with your parents' terry robes . . . pretending they were strapless gowns . . . and we'd stuff the tops with socks and tie the belts underneath . . ."

"Uh huh."

"And remember when we decided to cook dinner for my parents and we burned the bottoms of the pots?"

"Uh huh."

"And that day your new mattress came . . ." I began, trying to laugh. "Remember how we jumped up and down on it pretending it was a trampoline?"

"All of that was a long time ago, Steph . . ."

"I know . . . but don't you ever think about all the fun we used to have?"

"Not that much." She rolled over in bed.

I bit my lip, scared I might cry. I thought, Rachel doesn't want to be my best friend anymore. She probably wants to be best friends with Stacey Green.

Burt snuggled next to my legs. His purring put me to sleep. In the middle of the night he and Harry must have changed places because when I woke up on Saturday morning Harry was next to me and Burt was gone.

Rachel was already dressed and sitting at her desk.

"What are you doing up so early?" I asked. "It's Saturday."

"I like to get my homework out of the way on Saturday morning," Rachel said. "Then I have the rest of the weekend free to enjoy myself."

I rolled over thinking that I'm just the opposite. I always let my homework go until Sunday night. Rachel and I are opposites in so many ways.

By the time we went down to breakfast Mr. and Mrs. Robinson were getting ready to leave. Every Saturday morning they go for a hike in Devil's Den. If there's snow they take their cross-country skis. I wished my parents would find something to do together.

Mrs. Robinson was tying up her boots. "It's

good to have you here, Steph . . . you've been such a stranger lately."

What did she mean by that? "It's just that junior high keeps us so busy," I said.

Mr. Robinson kind of patted my head. "Don't let yourself get so busy you forget your friends."

I looked at Rachel but she was slicing a banana into her cereal.

"So I'll pick you up at the bank around five," Mr. Robinson said to us, as he wrapped a plaid scarf around his neck.

"We'll be there," Rachel said.

After breakfast Rachel changed the litter in Burt and Harry's box, then she cleaned her room. She dusted everything and vacuumed everywhere, including under her bed. She sprayed Windex on her mirror and the insides of her windows. She rearranged all her dresser drawers and made sure her closet was perfect.

"This must be the cleanest, neatest room in Palfrey's Pond," I said, "maybe even in all of Fairfield County."

"I like my room to be clean," Rachel said.

"Is Stacey Green like you?"

"What do you mean?"

"You know . . . does she clean her room and keep her drawers and closet the way you do?"

"Stacey is basically neat and organized, but not like me."

Rachel was lining up the photos on her dresser. One of them was the picture in the purple leather frame, the one Alison had given to us for Christmas. She held it for a minute before setting it back in its place. We look so happy in that picture, I thought. If only it could be that way again. "Rachel . . ." I began.

"What?"

I wanted to ask if she liked me anymore but I couldn't. So I just shook my head and said, "It's almost twelve-thirty. We should get going. Alison will be waiting for us."

36

Something Wild

All the stores in town were having mid-winter
sales. I suggested that we go to Enchantment
first because they don't have three-way mirrors.
I hate three-way mirrors. At Enchantment there
are no mirrors in the dressing rooms. If you
want to see how you look you have to come out
onto the floor. In some ways that's just as embarrassing because the sales people stand around
saying how great you look even when you don't.

I liked the first outfit I tried—a dark green
skirt and top, made of something that felt like
sweatshirt material. The skirt swirled around and
the top had a lacy collar and little animals march-
ing up and down the sleeves.

"This is it!" I announced, taking a quick look

at myself in the full-length mirror. "I'm all set for the dance."

"But, Steph . . ." Rachel said, "it's the first thing you've tried. Who knows what you might see someplace else?"

"I like it," I told her, "and it's a good price. I'll have enough left to buy shoes."

"You're just trying to avoid having to make a decision later," Rachel said.

"I am not!" Actually, I've always been the type of shopper who buys the first thing that looks good and Rachel knows it. I save a lot of time and trouble that way, plus I don't have to keep changing my clothes in stuffy dressing rooms.

"She's not going to find anything more becoming," the dark-haired saleswoman said to Rachel, as if Rachel were my mother.

"And that color was made for her," the blonde saleswoman added, trying to convince her.

I loved the way they were discussing me as if I wasn't there. On my way back to the dressing room I said, "I'm the one who's going to wear it and *I'm* completely satisfied!"

When I came out of the dressing room Rachel was trying on some gold knitted thing and the saleswomen were raving about it. Alison and I smiled at each other. "I'm glad you're taking that outfit," she said to me. "It looked great on you."

Rachel tried on everything in the store but

couldn't find anything wild enough so we headed down the street. We went to three more stores and at each of them Rachel asked a salesperson to hold aside a skirt or a top for her. She kept a list of who was holding what, the way she had the day we'd shopped for Alison's room.

Alison already had her outfit for the Ground Hog Day dance. All she needed was a camisole and tights to go under the gauzy blue skirt and shirt. She found them at Underpinnings. She was so sure of her size she didn't even bother to try them on.

After that we had to pee. The stores in town won't let you use their bathrooms. They claim they're for employees only. And the restaurants also give you a hard time unless you're eating there. Lucky for us there's a very nice, clean bathroom at Going Places, Mom's travel agency. It's even got lemon scented soap and pretty paper towels to dry your hands. I felt a little funny because Mom wasn't there, but I knew no one in the office would mind.

The chimes rang as I opened the door. Business looked good. Three clients were talking to agents and two more were waiting. Mom says that during January and February people start dreaming about spending a week in a warm and sunny place.

"Well . . . well . . ." Craig said, coming forward

to greet us. "Look what the wind blew in. I missed you this morning, Stephanie. I had to do all the filing myself."

"I'm glad to know you appreciate my hard work."

"I do . . . I do . . . I can hardly wait until you come back next Saturday."

"I won't be here next Saturday. Next Saturday is my birthday."

"I don't know . . ." he said. "You take a lot of time off. I guess when your mother owns the business you can get away with anything."

Alison nudged me. She really had to go. I said, "Actually, we came to use the . . ." I don't know why I had trouble saying *bathroom*. I say it all the time.

Rachel finished the sentence for me. "The facilities," she said to Craig.

As soon as Rachel said that Alison got a fit of the giggles and once she gets started, forget it! In a minute she had me laughing, too. Even Craig couldn't keep a straight face. But Rachel was annoyed and in the bathroom she said, "Are you two ever going to act your age?"

When we left Mom's office we hit four stores in a row. At the last one, Class Act, we ran into Amber Ackbourne and two of her friends. "We're shopping for the dance," Amber told us.

"So are we," Alison said.

Amber had on the same gold knitted thing Rachel had tried at Enchantment and her friends were oohing and aahing over how great she looked. Personally, I thought she looked as silly as Rachel had. "I wonder if Max will like me in this?" she said, posing in front of the mirror.

"Max?" Rachel said.

"Yes . . . he's the new boy in our homeroom and he's *sooo* cute. I may dance with him all night."

Rachel just stood here, with her mouth half opened.

"Haven't you heard?" I said, setting the record straight. "Max likes Rachel."

Amber turned away from the mirror and faced Rachel. "Is that true?"

"Of course it's true!" I said.

"I'm asking Rachel, not you," Amber said.

Rachel mumbled something.

"What?" Amber asked.

"I *said* it could be true," Rachel told her.

"*Could be* isn't the same as *definitely*," one of Amber's friends said.

And the other one said, "Just wait until he sees you in that gold sweater, Amber."

"I don't steal other people's boyfriends," Amber said.

"He's not exactly my boyfriend," Rachel said.

That was a really stupid thing for Rachel to

admit. So I had to set the record straight again. "He may not be her boyfriend but you should see them in the cafeteria."

Alison nodded but she didn't speak.

"You have the same lunch period as Max?" Amber asked Rachel.

"Yes," Rachel said, "but Max is a free person. He can dance with anyone he wants." She grabbed my sleeve. "We've got to go now."

"But we haven't see anything here," I said.

"We've seen enough!" Rachel spoke through clenched teeth.

"'Bye . . ." Amber called. "See you in school on Monday."

Outside, Rachel walked very fast. Alison and I had to hurry to keep up with her.

"How could you tell her that?" Rachel finally asked me.

"Tell her what?"

"That Max likes me."

"It's true, isn't it?"

"Even if it is, you had no business blabbing it to her."

"I wasn't about to let her think she can have any boy she wants," I said.

"Max is *my* business, not yours!"

"Come on, Rachel," Alison said, "Steph didn't mean anything . . . she was just trying to help."

Rachel marched down the street to Ollie's, a

store that's much too expensive for us. We never go there, even to browse. But Rachel went inside and announced to the saleswoman, "I want something really wild!"

The saleswoman was tall and thin. She was wearing a suede skirt, a denim shirt and boots. She had about twenty strands of beads around her neck. Her hair was bright red and frizzed around her face. She looked exactly the way I imagine Rachel wants to look at the Ground Hog Day dance. The name pin on her pocket said *Glory*.

"I guess I'm not quite sure what you mean by wild," Glory said to Rachel. "Because what's wild to you might not be wild to me and vice versa . . . if you get my point."

I thought about Mom's earrings and wondered if she was having a wild time in New York.

"So are we talking formally wild or informally wild?" Glory asked.

"Informally wild," Rachel said. "It's for a school dance."

"Hmmm . . ." Glory studied Rachel. "What size jeans . . . 28 long?"

"How did you know that?" Rachel asked.

"It's my job," Glory said, walking across the store to a rack of pants. She flipped through, pulled off a pair of white pants and handed them to Rachel. "While you're trying these I'll see what we have in wild tops. Do you want a covered or a bare look?"

"Not too bare," Rachel said, "but a little bare would be okay."

We followed Rachel into the dressing room. Alison sat on the floor, cross-legged, and I stood in the corner, trying not to block Rachel's view of herself in the three-way mirror. She pulled on the white pants, then turned round and round, examining herself from every angle.

That's when I noticed the label. "Oh-oh," I said, "they're designer jeans."

"So?" Rachel asked.

"So . . . your mother doesn't let you buy designer jeans."

"What are you . . . my conscience?"

"I'm just reminding you."

"I don't need you to remind me!"

"But your mother will see the label."

"If I decide to buy them," Rachel said, "which I haven't . . . I'll cut off the label."

"You'd lie to your own mother?"

"You're a good one to talk about lying!"

"What's that supposed to mean?"

"Forget it."

"No, I don't want to forget it."

Rachel spun around. "Okay, fine . . ." She pointed her finger at me. "You told us your mother went to Venice on business!"

"That's true."

"No, that's not true."

"What does she mean?" Alison asked me.

But Rachel didn't give me a chance to answer. "I mean that Stephanie has been lying to us since the beginning of the school year and I'm getting sick of it!"

"Lying?" Alison said.

"I haven't been lying!" Why was Rachel doing this to me?

"Her parents are separated," she told Alison. "They've been separated since the summer. They're probably going to get a divorce."

"No!" I said. "They're not getting divorced. It's a trial separation . . . that's why I didn't tell you!"

"Oh, please!" Rachel's yellow sweater had crept halfway up her middle. "You say you want to know everything about your friends' lives but when it comes to your own you don't see anything you don't want to see. You don't face reality. You live in some kind of sick fantasy world!"

"If anybody's sick around here it's you!" I cried. "You and your perfect room and your perfect grades and your perfect flute and . . ."

Rachel sucked in her breath. "When are you going to grow up?" she hissed.

"When I feel like it!"

"Stop it!" Alison covered her ears with her hands.

"This has nothing to do with you," Rachel yelled at her. "So just stay out of it."

"Don't tell her what to do!" I shouted. "You don't rule the world!"

Alison began to cry.

"Oh . . . you're both such babies!" Rachel yelled. "It's impossible to be friends with such insensitive, immature babies!"

"And it's just as impossible to be friends with somebody who thinks she knows everything . . . even when she doesn't!"

Rachel lunged and for a second I thought she was going to punch me. So I grabbed her first, by the arm, and I yelled, "Why don't you take your big brain and just shove it!"

She shook free of me and shouted, "And why don't you stay home and play Spit for the rest of your life like the big baby you are!"

"Girls!" Glory opened the curtain to the dressing room. "This is very unbecoming behavior. I'll have to ask you to leave if . . ."

"You don't have to ask me," I told her, "because I'm on my way!" I stormed out of the dressing room.

"I'm never speaking to you again!" Rachel yelled after me.

"That's the best news I've heard all day!" I yelled back.

Several customers stared at me as I ran through the store and out the glass door. Let them stare, I thought. Who cares? I had had enough of Rachel Robinson. This proved that not only wasn't she my best friend, she wasn't even my *friend*.

I didn't realize I'd left my jacket on the floor of the dressing room until Alison came through the door carrying it. I didn't even know I was crying until she handed me a tissue. Then I felt the hot tears on my face and the drip from my nose freezing on my upper lip and chin.

"I'm sorry about your parents," Alison said, softly. "I had no idea."

"It's not your problem," I told her.

"Yes, it is," she said, draping my jacket over my shoulders.

At five, Alison and I went to the bank where we had arranged to meet Mr. Robinson. If I had had enough money I'd have called a cab. But I'd spent my last few dollars buying shoes for the dance.

Rachel was already there, waiting for her father. She was carrying two packages. I wondered what she'd bought. As soon as she saw us she turned away. When her father pulled up she got into the front seat of the car and Alison and I got into the back.

"Well," Mr. Robinson said, eyeing our packages. "I see you've had a successful afternoon."

When we didn't respond he said, "I guess you're tired out. Shopping will do it to you every time."

When we still didn't answer he laughed and said, "Better you than me. I'd rather do anything than shop." After that I think he got the message and he didn't say anything more.

When we got to Rachel's I whispered to Alison, "Can I stay at your house tonight?"

"Sure," Alison said.

"I'll get my things and be right over."

Rachel ran into the house, tore upstairs and locked herself in the bathroom.

I tossed my things into my canvas bag, found a sheet of paper in Rachel's desk drawer and wrote a note:

Dear Mrs. Robinson:

Thank you for inviting me to spend the weekend. I can't stay over tonight for very personal reasons. I hope you understand. If you don't, you can ask Rachel. I will be at Alison's, if my mother calls.

Sincerely,
Stephanie

37

Personal Stuff

I would never forgive Rachel for the horrible things she said about me. My parents' separation was none of her business. Besides, what did she know about how I was feeling inside? Which proved that Rachel Robinson was the one who was immature and insensitive, not me!

Mom came back from New York on Sunday afternoon but I didn't tell her about Rachel and me until we sat down to supper. Then, while she dished out tomato-rice soup, I said, "Rachel and I had a fight. We're never speaking to each other again!"

Mom said, "I'm sure you can patch it up if you try."

"I don't want to try."

Mom covered the pot of soup and bit into a cracker. "That's not like you, Steph. After all, you and Rachel have been best friends since second grade."

"Well, we're not anymore!"

"But you've got so much in common."

"No," I said, "we don't have anything in common. That's the problem."

"You shared your childhoods," Mom said. "You'll always have that in common."

"That's not enough!"

"It's stupid to fight with your friends," Bruce said, slurping his soup.

"Rachel is *not* my friend."

"But she was . . . before you had the fight . . . right?"

"Before we had the fight doesn't count," I told Bruce.

"That's how wars get started," he said.

"Nobody is talking about war!" I shouted.

"Calm down, Steph . . ." Mom said, "and eat your soup before it gets cold."

When I got into bed that night I went over the fight in my mind again, trying to figure out how it had started. But all I could remember was the part about the designer jeans, and the shouting, and the tears. I had trouble falling asleep. When I finally did, I dreamed I was at the Ground Hog Day dance, naked. *Baby . . . baby*

. . . *baby*, Rachel sang, taunting me. Everyone else laughed and pointed. Finally, Mrs. Remo covered me with her coat.

When Dad called the next night I told him that Rachel and I were never speaking again.

He said, "You two will make up in no time."

"We will not."

"Want to bet?" Dad asked.

"No."

"Well, I do. I'll bet five dollars that before your birthday you and Rachel are best friends again."

"My birthday's this Friday, so you're definitely going to lose."

"I'll take that chance."

Parents always think they know so much about their kids when really, they hardly know a thing.

"So," Dad said, "how was Mom's weekend in New York?"

"Why don't you ask her yourself?" I thrust the phone at Mom, who was relaxing at the kitchen table, sipping tea and reading the newspaper.

"Yes, Steve . . ." Mom said, taking the phone, "everyone's fine."

I began to peel the label off the jar of mayonnaise that was still sitting on the counter. If I'm really careful I can sometimes peel labels off in one piece, which feels almost as good as peeling sunburned skin.

"A fling?" Mom said into the phone. "No, I

did not have a fling in New York . . . not that it would be any of your business if I had."

I put the mayonnaise jar in the refrigerator and tried to sneak out of the kitchen but I didn't make it. "Stephanie!" Mom called, as she hung up the phone. "Did you tell Dad I was going to New York to have a fling?"

"I might have mentioned something about that," I said. "And by the way . . . how was Carla's party?"

"Don't try to change the subject," Mom said and I could tell by the tone of her voice she was serious. "You had no business discussing my social life behind my back."

"Dad was jealous, wasn't he?"

"This is a marriage, not some junior high romance," Mom said. "We've got to work it out ourselves."

"I don't see why I can't help."

"Because you don't have the power to make it turn out the way you want . . . you'll only wind up disappointed. Do you understand?"

"No!" I shouted, as I ran out of the kitchen and up the stairs. If you asked me, Mom and Dad were behaving just like Jeremy and Dana. I slammed my bedroom door and threw myself on my bed, on top of my stuffed animals. I hated the way Rachel, and now Mom, accused me of butting into their social lives when all I was trying to do was help. I lay there for a long time, crying. I was sure Mom would come to my room to apologize, but she didn't.

Word gets around fast at school. By lunchtime on Tuesday everyone knew that Rachel and I weren't speaking. On the bus Rachel sat with Dana, as far from Alison and me as possible. And in the cafeteria she sat at Stacey Green's table. I saw her fooling around with Max, too.

Kara Klaff asked, "What'd you two fight about anyway?"

"Personal stuff," I answered.

Miri Levine said, "Do you think you'll make up soon, or what?"

"Never," I told her.

Amber Ackbourne came up to me in homeroom. "I can't believe that you and Rachel aren't speaking. I mean, you and Rachel have been friends forever. I hope it didn't have anything to do with Max or that gold sweater I bought for the dance."

"Don't flatter yourself," I said. "It didn't."

After school Alison said, "Everybody's asking if I'm on your side or Rachel's. They don't know she called me an insensitive, immature baby, too. I hate fights!"

"It wasn't my idea to have ⎯⎯⎯" I reminded her.

"I know," Alison said. "I was the⎯⎯⎯⎯ remember?"

We squeezed hands and I thought⎯⎯⎯ lucky I am to have Alison for my best friend. Because if Rachel had been my only best friend imagine how lonely I'd feel now. As lonely as Rachel would feel if she didn't have Stacey Green.

That night it began to snow and by the time I went to bed it was coming down hard. I had another bad dream. This time Rachel and I were walking along a highway but there was no traffic. Then, suddenly, a speeding car came out of nowhere and headed straight for us. We tried to run but our feet wouldn't move. The car smashed into Rachel. Her body flew up in the air, sailed across the highway and landed with a thud. I raced to her side but it was too late. When the police came they arrested me even though I hadn't done a thing. The policeman who handcuffed me looked exactly like Benjamin Moore. He said, *You planned the whole thing, didn't you?* I screamed, *No! No!* and woke up shaking and covered with sweat.

Bruce raced into my room. "What was that?"

a bad dream," I said.

. ary?"

"Sort of . . ."

"About the bomb?"

"No."

"You want me to stay with you?"

"I'm okay now."

He went to my window and looked out. "It's still snowing. I hope school is closed tomorrow."

"Yeah . . . we could use a snow day."

"I guess I'll go back to bed now."

When he got to my door I said, "Bruce . . ."

"Yeah?"

"Thanks for coming to my room."

"That's okay," he said. "I know what it's like to have bad dreams."

What's weird is, Bruce hasn't had a nightmare since he won second place in the poster contest. Mom says he feels better now that he knows he's not the only one who cares. He's even been invited to become an honorary member of two national organizations that work for peace.

It was still snowing when we woke up on Wednesday morning. School was closed. Bruce and I whooped for joy, then went back to sleep.

The snow stopped and the sun came out around eleven. Bruce and his friend, David, built a snowman in our yard. I tied a scarf around his neck and set Dad's brown felt hat on his head.

Seeing the hat on the snowman reminded me of the old days, when Dad would play with us in the snow. I wonder if we'll ever do that again.

After lunch Alison and I went down to the pond to skate. Rachel was there, too, with Dana, but she just gave me a haughty look. So I gave her one back. I learned that word from Rachel. It means arrogant, which means hoity-toity, which means thinking you are great, which definitely fits Rachel. While I was showing off, skating backwards, I tripped and fell. Alison had to help me to my feet. She sat on a log with me for a while, until the pain in my backside went away. After that I stuck to ordinary skating and when Rachel did a series of figure eights, I didn't act impressed like everyone else at the pond.

Mom had gone to the office for a few hours that afternoon and when she got home, around five, I was sitting in the den nibbling a bowl of carrot sticks and reading. I'd decided to try *Gone With the Wind* after all, proving that Rachel isn't the only person in seventh grade who can read grown-up books. Mom changed into her exercise clothes and shoved her Jazzercise tape into the VCR. When the leader came on the screen Mom began her warmup stretches.

I put down my book. "I think I'll try that today," I said, standing behind Mom and copying her movements.

When we got to the number where the leader says, "Okay . . . now I want you to make believe you're punching someone you really can't stand! Remember . . . it's a lot better to punch the air than someone you know," I punched as hard as I could. First to the right, then to the left. *Take that* . . . I thought, *and that!* Punch . . . punch . . . punch . . . until Mom touched my arm and said, "The number's over, Steph. You can stop punching now."

38

Slow Dancing

A package arrived from Dad on Friday. I took it to my room. The card showed an older elephant talking to a younger one. It said *Happy Birthday to someone young enough to enjoy it but old enough to know better*. Under that, Dad had written, *Wish I could be with you to celebrate your thirteenth! Love, Dad*. I turned it over to see if it was made of recycled paper. It was. I unwrapped the box and opened it slowly. Inside was an amethyst heart on a gold chain. Amethyst is my birthstone.

I ran downstairs. Mom was fixing an early dinner because the Ground Hog Day dance was starting at seven-thirty. "Look what Dad sent for my birthday," I said, dangling the necklace under her nose.

Mom glanced up from the chicken and vegetables she was stir-frying. "Very pretty."

"You think he picked it out himself?" I asked.

"I hope so," Mom said.

"Me too . . . because if Iris picked it out I'll never wear it. I'll flush it down the toilet first!"

"Really, Steph . . ." Mom laughed. But I think she was glad I said that.

"How would it look with my green outfit?"

"When you get dressed for the dance you can try it and see," Mom said.

"But how can I wear this *plus* my bee-sting necklace?"

"There are no bees at night," Mom said, "especially in the winter."

"Then I guess I'll wear Dad's necklace tonight and tomorrow, when I go to New York, I'll wear Gran Lola's." I paused for a second. "And I'll wear my new boots tomorrow, too." I added that because Mom had given me a pair of cowboy boots for my birthday. They're something like the ones Marcella wore to the movies the night I saw her with Jeremy Dragon, except mine are a soft grayish color and Marcella's are white. I didn't get my own phone. Oh, well . . . there's always next year.

"Steph . . ." Mom began.

"I really love the boots you gave me!" I said. I

didn't want to hurt Mom's feelings, making her think I liked Dad's present better.

But Mom had something else on her mind. "Don't you think we should ask Rachel if she needs a ride to the dance tonight?" she asked.

"No!"

Rachel had written a note to my mother:

Dear Mrs. Hirsch,

Due to a change in plans I won't be able to go to New York on Saturday to help celebrate Stephanie's birthday.

Sincerely,
Rachel Robinson

"I talked to Nell today," Mom said.

"You called Mrs. Robinson?"

"She called me. Rachel is suffering."

"Good," I said. "Rachel deserves to suffer!"

"Stephanie . . . I'm surprised at you. Where's your compassion?"

"It's my birthday," I said. "Where's her compassion? Besides, you don't know the terrible things she said about me."

"Maybe she's sorry," Mom said

"Then let her tell me herself."

The gym looked great. Besides crepe-paper streamers and balloons in different colors, huge letters spelling out *Ground Hog Day* were strung across one wall. The other walls were covered with murals of ground hogs looking for their shadows. My two favorite teachers, Mrs. Remo and Mr. Diamond, were chaperones, along with the other seventh grade homeroom teachers.

When Alison and I got there Eric Macaulay, Peter Klaff and Max Wilson were already gathered around the refreshment table, stuffing their faces with cookies and fruit punch. Nobody was dancing yet.

We were there for at least ten minutes before Rachel came in with Stacey Green. She was dressed all in white. I couldn't tell if her white pants were the designer jeans she'd tried at Ollie's on the day of the fight, or not. But I know we hadn't seen her top, which was pleated and shaped like a lamp shade. She had a white flower in her hair, too. A gardenia, I think. I was too far away to smell it. She didn't look like a person who was suffering at all.

We stood around for a while, girls talking to girls and boys talking to boys, until Amber Ackbourne dragged Max Wilson out to the middle of the floor, to dance. Then Toad asked Alison to dance and soon all the boys were cutting in on each other to get their turns with Alison. All but Eric Macaulay. He just watched. So I was really shocked when he suddenly grabbed my hand and said, "Come on, El Chunko . . . let's dance!"

"My name is Stephanie!" I reminded him.

"Yeah . . . yeah."

Eric surprised me. He actually knew how to dance. And even though we didn't touch because it wasn't a slow number, he managed to dance me over to where Peter Klaff was standing. When we were right in front of Peter, Eric shoved me at him. "Catch . . ." Eric called to Peter, laughing. I almost fell over but Peter caught me. He didn't let go of me right away either.

Next, Eric grabbed Rachel around the waist. He only came up to her chest but he danced her over to Max and Amber. When he was right up close he shoved Rachel at Max, the way he had shoved me at Peter. Rachel went flying, nearly knocking over Amber. Eric rescued Amber and before she knew what was happening he danced her away, leaving Max and Rachel together. Then Eric danced Amber over to Alison and shoved her at Alison's partner. Finally, Eric had Alison to himself.

"I can't believe this!" I said to Peter, who was standing with his hands in his pockets.

"He planned the whole thing," Peter said, "and it worked." He looked at me. "So . . . you want to dance?"

"Sure."

"Okay . . . there's just one problem."

"What's that?" I asked.

"I don't know how," he said.

"I'll teach you." A slow song was playing. "Put your arm around my waist," I told him.

"I know that part," Peter said. "The part I don't know is what to do with my feet."

"Try this," I said. "Forward, to the side, together . . . backward, to the side, together." I kind of dragged Peter around with me.

Peter kept repeating, "Forward, to the side, together . . . backward, to the side, together." And soon he said, "Hey, we're dancing." Sometimes we stepped on each other's feet, but so what? We danced for six numbers, fast and slow, before Peter said, "I drank a lot of punch. I've got to go . . ."

"Me too."

"Meet you back here in five minutes or less," he said, pushing the timer on his stop watch.

I headed for the girls' room mainly because my pantyhose were falling down. Probably I'd bought the wrong size. I'd had trouble figuring out the height and weight chart printed on the back of the package. Two other girls were in there. One of them, Emily ⟨...⟩ from my math class. She was p⟨...⟩ We greeted each other, then I ⟨...⟩

When I pulled down my pants⟨...⟩ brown stain inside. What's this? I ⟨...⟩ it be? No . . . probably not. But i⟨...⟩ what is it? By the time I flushed the ⟨...⟩ I knew for sure because there were a few drops of menstrual blood in there. Imagine that . . , my period on my thirteenth birthday! I had to think fast. "Emily . . ." I called. "Are you still out there?"

"Yes."

"Could you pass me some paper towels?"

"What for?" Emily asked.

"I've got my period," I said, trying it out. It sounded so grown-up!

"Don't you want a pad?"

"I don't have any money with me . . . do you?"

"No, but I could go ask somebody."

"That's okay," I said. "Just pass me the paper towels."

"Here . . ." she said, shoving a whole stack under the door.

"Thanks." I stuck half a dozen of them inside my pants but they felt hard and rough against me. Still, they were better than nothing. I couldn't wait to tell Alison what had happened! But when I got back to the gym she was dancing with Eric

...d Peter was waiting for me at the ...ent table. "I thought you fell in," he ..., checking his watch. "You were gone nine minutes, seventeen seconds."

We started dancing again but I couldn't help thinking: Suppose the paper towels aren't enough? Suppose it gets on my skirt and Peter says, *What's that . . . your period?*

"You're not doing *forward, to the side, together* the way you were before," Peter said.

"Oh, sorry . . ." How could I concentrate on dancing at a time like this? I tried to get Alison's attention. I beckoned to her but she thought I was waving and she waved back. She and Eric never stopped dancing. Finally I broke away from Peter and said, "I just remembered . . . I've got to tell Mrs. Remo something."

"Now?"

"Yes."

"Are you trying to get rid of me?" Peter asked.

"No . . . this has nothing to do with you."

"Okay." He pushed the button on his watch again. "You've got five minutes . . . starting now!"

I went over to Mrs. Remo and asked if I could talk to her in private. She put her arm around me. "Are the boys giving you a hard time?" she asked.

"No." I wondered why she thought that. "It's my . . ." Then for some reason I started to laugh.

"What?" Mrs. Remo asked.

"I just got my period and I don't have any . . ." I couldn't stop laughing.

"Is this your first time?"

I nodded because I was laughing too hard to speak.

"Let's see what we can do." Mrs. Remo went to the girls' room with me, deposited the right coins in the machine on the wall and handed me a pad. "Just peel off the bottom and stick it to your panties," she whispered. "I'll wait here . . . just in case."

I tried to stop laughing. I'm not the type to get giggling fits, like Alison. I attached the pad to my pants, pulled everything up again and came out of the booth just as Alison burst into the girls' room. "Are you okay?" she asked. "Peter said something's going on."

"I'm fine," I told her. "I just got my period."

"Oh, Steph . . " Alison hugged me. "That's so exciting! And on your birthday, too."

"It's your birthday?" Mrs. Remo asked.

"Yes. I'm thirteen today."

Mrs. Remo also gave me a hug, which was kind of embarrassing. "Happy Birthday, Stephanie!"

Peter and Eric were waiting for Alison and me. "That was twelve minutes, four seconds," Peter said. I wished he hadn't gotten a stop watch for Christmas.

Mrs. Remo went to the microphone and tapped it. "Attention everyone . . ." she said, "I want to make an announcement. I just found out something special about Stephanie Hirsch."

Oh, no! I thought. She's going to announce my period to the entire seventh grade. This was worse than the dream I'd had about the dance, where I was naked and Mrs. Remo had to cover me with her coat. I felt my face turn hot. I felt dizzy. I'm going to pass out, I thought. I reached for Peter's arm to steady myself, which he took to mean I wanted to hold hands.

Mrs. Remo began to speak. "Today . . ."

"No!" I called in a weak voice, hoping to stop Mrs. Remo. But Peter thought *no* meant I didn't want to hold hands and he quickly moved a step away from me.

"Today is Stephanie's thirteenth birthday," Mrs. Remo said. "Let's all wish her a very happy one." The whole class began to sing and my dizzy spell passed. I glanced over at Rachel, who was standing close to Max Wilson. She wasn't singing. Our eyes met for a minute before she turned away. I remembered my promise, that she and Alison would be the first to know when I got my period. But promises to someone who isn't your friend anymore don't count.

During the last half hour of the dance Rachel and Max were wrapped together, barely moving in time to the music. Her head was buried in his neck and his eyes were half-closed. They were definitely the most intense couple at the dance.

When the music ended there was a dash for the coat room. As soon as we found our coats Peter and I went outside. It was a cold, clear night and Peter pointed toward the sky. "Look . . . there's Orion."

When I looked up he kissed me. "Happy Birthday, Steph."

I was so surprised I couldn't think of a thing to say.

"I never did that before," he confessed.

"Neither did I."

"Let's do it again," he said.

"Okay." This time I was careful to keep my lips closed. I wasn't taking any chances that our braces would get stuck together. I didn't get the same kind of tingles from kissing Peter as I do from standing close to Jeremy Dragon or pretending that Benjamin Moore is my boyfriend, but kissing him felt warm and friendly.

Peter left as soon as he spotted his mother's car. I stood alone for a minute, thinking about everything that had happened to me tonight.

"Oh, there you are," Alison said. "I had the best time! Eric kissed me good night."

"Peter kissed me, too."

"Eric kissed me twice."

"Same here."

"Do you think they planned it?" Alison asked.

"Did he tell you to look up at Orion?"

"Yes," she said.

"Then they planned it."

"So . . . who cares?" we said at the same time. And then we laughed.

Mom couldn't believe I got my period. She was more excited than I was. "Come on, Mom . . ." I said, "it happens to every girl sooner or later."

"I know," she said, sitting on my bed after the dance, "but it's very special when it happens to your own daughter. I'm so proud of you, Steph!"

"Just because I got my period?"

"No . . . just because." She was getting kind of teary and had to stop to blow her nose. "I just wish you and Rachel would make up. Nell stopped by tonight while you were at the dance. She left a package for you. I'll go get it."

Mom came back to my room with a box wrapped in silver paper, tied with a purple ribbon. I opened the card. *With love to the birthday girl, from all the Robinsons*, it said in Mrs. Robinson's handwriting. Inside the box was a long, white Victorian nightgown, the kind the girl in *The Nutcracker* wears. I've always wanted one. I held it up for Mom to see.

"It's beautiful," she said. "Why don't you phone and thank them."

"I'll write a note instead," I said.

I called Dad the next morning to thank him for my birthday necklace. But I forgot about the time difference and I woke him. "Should I call back later?" I asked.

"No . . . that's okay." He sounded groggy. I hoped Iris wasn't there. "What time is it, anyway?"

"It's almost ten here so I guess it's almost seven there."

He yawned. "I wanted to get up early today."

"I called to thank you for the necklace. It's beautiful. I love amethyst."

"I'm glad. How was the dance?"

"It was great!" I thought about telling him I got my period but decided against it. I didn't want him blabbing it to Iris. It was none of her business. "By the way . . . you owe me five dollars."

"I do?"

"Yes . . . you lost your bet."

"What bet?"

"That Rachel and I would be best friends again by my birthday."

At eleven, Alison, Bruce and I took the train to New York. I asked Bruce to take Rachel's place because it was too late to invite another friend from school. And, in a way, I was glad to take him. Bruce can be very good company. Also, he made a beautiful decoupage box for my birthday. Mom said he'd been working on it secretly for a month.

Mrs. Robinson

The following week there was another snowstorm and school was closed again. I spent the afternoon at Alison's and as I walked home the sun began to set, turning the sky pink and purple. I breathed in the clean, fresh smell of the new snow. It had been a perfect afternoon. I began to hum a song I'd heard on Alison's stereo. As I passed Rachel's house I noticed Mrs. Robinson, trying to shovel her car out of a snowdrift. I should have walked the other way around the pond, I thought. I bent my head and walked faster but Mrs. Robinson saw me anyway.

"Steph . . ." she called.

I looked up as if I was really surprised. "Oh—hi, Mrs. Robinson. I didn't see you."

She came toward me, carrying her snow shovel.

"You need a hand with your car?" I asked.

"No, it's hopeless," she said. "I'll have to wait for the plow." She kind of leaned on her shovel. "Thanks for your note. It was very sweet."

"I really like the nightgown," I told her.

"Rachel said you would."

I wish she hadn't said Rachel's name. Every time I hear it I get a pain in my stomach.

"Stephanie . . ." Mrs. Robinson began, and I knew from the serious tone of her voice I didn't want to hear what was coming. "What happened between you and Rachel?"

"You'll have to ask her," I said.

"I have . . . but she won't tell me."

I didn't know what to say so I just stood there, wishing Mrs. Robinson hadn't seen me.

"Surely you two can talk it over and make peace," Mrs. Robinson said. "I know Rachel wants to be your friend. I know how important you are to her."

I looked away, to the Robinsons' house. I thought I saw Rachel, watching us from her bedroom window.

"She's terribly hurt, Steph. You know how sensitive she is. You know how much she needs you."

"She needs me?" I said. Imagine Rachel needing anyone!

"Yes," Mrs. Robinson said, "she needs you very much. She depends on you."

"Did she tell you that?" I asked.

"She doesn't have to tell me. I can see it. Isn't there anything I can do to help the two of you get back together?"

I shook my head.

"Your parents' separation must be very hard on you and I don't mean to make it worse," Mrs. Robinson said.

I wanted to tell her to shut up, that she had no business discussing my parents' separation but she went right on talking. "Taking your anger out on Rachel isn't fair, Steph."

"That's what you think I'm doing?"

"Am I wrong?" Mrs. Robinson asked.

"Yes, you're wrong!" I said, choking up.

"Then I'm sorry." She tried to put her arm around me but I pulled away and began to run. As I got closer to my house I tripped and landed in a snowdrift, soaking my jeans.

"Can you believe Mrs. Robinson said that to me?" I asked Mom that night. "Can you believe she thinks I'm taking out my anger on Rachel? Have you ever heard such a stupid thing?"

"Maybe she's right," Mom said. "Maybe that is what's happening."

"Mom!"

"Hasn't this nonsense with Rachel gone on long enough? Why don't you apologize, Steph?"

"Me, apologize! For what? I wish you'd stop trying to get us back together!" I shouted. "This is *our* problem, not yours!" I ran upstairs and slammed my bedroom door. My perfect afternoon had been ruined!

Dad called a few days later. "I thought you'd want to know," he said, "as of May first I'm coming back to the New York office."

"What?" I asked, switching the phone from one ear to the other. "What did you say?"

"I'll be working out of the New York office beginning the first of May," Dad said, slowly, as if we didn't speak the same language.

"Is Iris coming with you?"

"Iris and I aren't seeing each other anymore."

This was news to me! "Since before or after my birthday?"

"Before," Dad said. "But look, Steph . . . I don't want you to blame yourself."

Blame myself? I thought.

"I know that kids always blame themselves for these things," Dad said.

They do?

"It wasn't your fault," Dad continued. "Iris

and I finally sat down and talked it over and we realized we have different priorities."

"So you broke up?"

"Please try not to feel guilty."

Feel guilty?

"There was a lot more to our decision than what happened at Christmas."

Oh . . . Christmas. So that's why he thought I'd feel guilty. My head was filled with questions. "Where will you live?" I asked. What I really meant was, *Will you and Mom get back together? Will you come home?* But it was too hard to come right out and say what was on my mind.

"I'll probably take an apartment in the city," Dad said, "at least in the beginning."

What did that mean? "So you'll be living in New York starting May first?"

"Yes," he said. "Life out here isn't what I expected. And I miss you and Bruce very much. Once I'm in New York we'll be able to see each other every week."

Every week? Did that mean he would come up here or Bruce and I would go to the city? My stomach started growling but I didn't feel hungry.

When I hung up I went to Mom's room. "Did you know Dad's coming back to the New York office?"

Mom was at her computer. "Yes," she said, quietly.

"And his fling with Iris is over, too."

"Yes," she said again.

"So what does it mean?" I asked.

"We don't know yet, Steph. We've still got a lot of thinking to do."

"But you might get back together . . . right?"

"Don't get your hopes up."

"But it's a possibility, isn't it?"

"I suppose it's a possibility . . . but it's not likely."

"I hate not knowing what's going to happen!" I shouted. "I'd almost rather know you're getting a divorce. I want it to be settled one way or the other so I can get used to the idea, so I can stop thinking about it."

"I'm not going to lie to you, Steph," Mom said. "We just don't know . . ."

"You're supposed to be grownups," I shouted at her, "so why can't you make up your minds?" I ran to my room and slammed the door.

This time Mom followed me. "I'm getting tired of your moody outbursts!" she shouted. "Other people live here too, you know. And it's time you showed some concern for their feelings."

"I show a lot of concern for Bruce's feelings!" I shouted back at her.

40

Killer Flu

In March everyone got the flu. Everyone but Alison and me. Rachel had it. Dana had it. Miri Levine and Peter Klaff have it and I think Eric Macaulay is coming down with it because he coughed all day today and fell asleep in home-room, with his head on his desk. Mrs. Remo says if we develop symptoms we should definitely not come to school. I heard her tell Mr. Diamond, "They're dropping like flies in my homeroom."

I called Peter to see how he was feeling.

"This flu is a killer," he said. "I cough half the night."

"Can't your mother give you something?"

"She's working on it."

"When are you coming back to school?"

"Not until I'm better, which at this rate means next fall."

"Well, cheer up," I told him. "You're not missing that much. Half the class is absent."

"Yeah . . . Mom says it's an epidemic."

"Probably I'll be next," I said.

"Then I'll call you."

"Deal," I said. The thing I like best about Peter is he's not just a boy, he's a friend.

When Alison called a few nights later, in tears, I figured it was to tell me that she had the flu, too. But instead she said, "This is an emergency." Her voice quivered. "I've got to see you right away."

"You want me to come over?" I asked. Never mind that it was close to nine on a school night and outside it was windy and raining. If Alison needed me I would go. That's what friends are for.

"I'll come to your house," Alison said.

"Did somebody die?" I asked, thinking of Sadie Wishnik.

"No . . ." Alison said, "nobody died."

"That's a relief."

Alison came to the kitchen door carrying her overnight bag in one hand and Maizie tucked under her other arm. This was the first time Alison had brought Maizie to our house. I won-

dered why she'd picked a rainy night
first visit. And how come she was carr
overnight bag.

Maizie shook herself off, then sniffed around
the kitchen.

Alison took off her wet slicker and hung it over
the back of a kitchen chair. Her eyes were red
and puffy.

"What's wrong?" I said.

"Where's your mother?"

"In her room. Why?"

"Where's Bruce?"

"He's upstairs too. What's going on?"

"What I have to say I have to say in private."

"Okay . . . fine."

"Can we get to your room without anyone
seeing us?"

"We can try," I said.

Alison grabbed Maizie and held her jaws together so she couldn't bark. We crept up the
stairs slowly and ducked into my room. Then
Maizie leaped out of Alison's arms and hid under
the dresser. Alison sat on the edge of my bed,
her hands clasped tightly in front of her. "My
mother is pregnant," she announced.

"No!"

"And they don't know how it happened."

"You mean it didn't happen in the usual way?"

rty years old and she's never
pregnant and now, all of a

ng!" I said.

an amazing."

going to do?"

"She's going to have it. She and Leon think it's
the greatest news they've ever heard. It doesn't
bother them that when the kid is my age Mom
will be fifty-three and Leon will be sixty-five."

I tried to picture Gena Farrell pregnant, but I
couldn't. I couldn't picture her old either.

"What about the series?" I asked.

"How can you think of a TV series at a time
like this?"

"I don't know. It just popped into my head."
I like Gena's new TV series. It's funny but not
silly. I watch it every Tuesday night. Maybe Leon
could give Franny—that's the name of the char-
acter Gena plays—a baby on the show. That
would be very interesting.

Alison was crying again. "Mom says she didn't
tell me until tonight because they just got the
results of the amniocentesis . . ."

"What's amniocentesis?" I asked.

"Some test they do on older women to make
sure the baby is okay. They even know what sex
it is."

"What?"

"It's a . . ." She shook her head. I sat beside her and put my arm around her shoulder. "It's a boy," she finally managed to say.

"So you'll have a younger brother, same as me."

"You don't get it, do you?" she cried. "This isn't anything like you and Bruce."

"Because you'll be thirteen years older?"

"No . . . because it will be *their* baby. Their *own* baby. Not some baby Gena adopted because she couldn't get pregnant. This baby will look like them."

"I hope it looks like Gena," I said. "Not that there's anything wrong with the way Leon looks . . . but Gena's a lot . . ." I stopped when I realized that wasn't what Alison meant. She meant this baby won't be Vietnamese.

"They won't need me anymore."

"Come on, Alison! I never saw a kid as loved as you."

"Until now! But who knows what's going to happen in July?"

I wanted to tell her about Dad and how he was coming back to the New York office on May first. I wanted to tell her that I don't know what's going to happen either. But it didn't feel like the right time to bring up my family problems.

"I'm going to France tomorrow," Alison said. "I'm going to find my biological mother."

"How?"

"There are ways."

"I think you're making a big mistake," I said.

We both heard the doorbell ring. Alison rushed to the window and looked out. "It's them," she whispered. "I'll hide in the closet."

"Alison, I wish you'd . . ."

"Shush . . ."

She was in the closet, with Maizie, when Mom opened my door. "Is Alison here?"

You could tell Alison was trying to keep Maizie from barking by the muffled sounds coming from the closet.

"Your parents are downstairs waiting, Alison," Mom said, as if nothing unusual was going on.

As soon as Mom was gone Alison opened the closet door and came out with Maizie in her arms. "I guess I'll go home now," she said. Her voice sounded hoarse. "I guess I'll wait until tomorrow to decide what to do."

"You look kind of funny," I told her.

"I feel kind of funny," she said. And then she just keeled over.

"Mom!" I called, "Come quick . . ."

Mom, Gena and Leon raced up the stairs. "Pumpkin!" Leon said. He lifted Alison onto my bed.

Gena felt her forehead. "She's burning up!"

"It's probably the flu," I told them. "The kids at school are dropping like flies."

"What's going on?" Bruce asked, standing in my doorway.

Alison opened her eyes. "My dog can talk," she said.

"What was that all about?" Mom asked, after Leon and Gena took Alison home.

"Family problems," I said.

"I hope it's nothing serious." Mom turned out the lamps in the living room.

"Gena's pregnant but no one's supposed to know. And Alison thinks once they have their own baby they won't love her anymore."

"Of course they will," Mom said, as we went upstairs.

"That's what I told her," I said. "I never saw a kid as loved as Alison."

"What about you and Bruce?" Mom followed me into my room.

I shrugged.

"You don't think we love you as much as they love Alison?"

"I don't know."

"Stephanie . . . of course we do!"

"Maybe."

"Just because we have disagreements from time to time doesn't mean we don't love each other," Mom said.

"I guess."

"I was tough on you that night, wasn't I?" Mom asked.

"What night?"

"That night I told you to think of other people's feelings."

"Oh . . . *that* night."

"From now on," Mom said, "if we have something to say we should say it. It's not good to hold in feelings . . . anger and resentment build up that way."

"Did you know I went to see the counselor at school?" I asked.

"No."

"Only one time . . . she wanted to help me with my problems but I told her I didn't have any. Rachel says I don't face reality."

"Is that what your fight was about?"

"That's part of it. Do you think I face reality?"

"I think you handle it in your own way. I don't see you hiding from the facts. I don't see you withdrawing."

"Sometimes I pretend everything's okay when it's not."

"So do I," Mom said. "That's how I make it through the day."

"We're a lot alike, aren't we?" I asked. "We're both optimists."

Mom hugged me. "We sure are."

41

Spring

It's been seven weeks since Rachel and I stopped speaking. At the bus stop in the morning she doesn't even look at me. She and Dana stand together, talking and laughing. Sometimes they talk so softly I can't hear what they're saying. I wish Alison would hurry and get better. I hate standing at the bus stop by myself. I've never felt so left out in my life. It's as if I'm invisible, as if I don't exist. Well, fine. Because as far as I'm concerned, Rachel Robinson doesn't exist either. Besides, I have more important things on my mind, such as what happens on May first when Dad starts working in New York?

I took Alison's homework assignments to her but the first three days she was too sick to do anything. Leon let me peek into her room. Seeing her like that, so small and pale with her eyes closed, frightened me. I guess Leon could tell because he said, "It looks worse than it is. She's going to be fine."

Later that week when I got to her house, Alison was sitting up in bed, sipping grape juice. "I feel a little better," she said, coughing.

"I can tell."

She held up a book—*What to Name the Baby*. "I'm trying to find a good name for him. You'd be amazed at how many names there are. So far Mom likes Alexander, Leon likes Edward and Sadie Wishnik likes Nelson . . ."

"Nelson?" I said.

"I know," Alison said, "it's terrible." She laughed a little but that made her start coughing again. "You better not come too close."

"I'm not afraid of catching it," I said. Actually, the idea of a week in bed, with Mrs. Greco making me cinnamon toast and camomile tea, didn't sound all that bad.

"It's good I didn't go to Paris after all," Alison said. "I'd have been stuck there with the flu."

"Yeah . . . and without Leon to take care of you."

"I've decided to wait and see what happens. Maybe it won't be that bad. And if it is, I can always leave after the baby is born."

"Right," I said. Maizie came in and jumped up on Alison's chair. "Guess what?" I asked, running my fingers along Maizie's back. "My father's coming back to work in New York."

"When?" Alison asked.

"May first."

"What's going to happen?"

"I wish I knew!"

"Well, at least you'll be able to see him whenever you want."

I nodded.

"Leon says you can feel spring in the air today," Alison said, lying back against her pillows. "I wish I could go outside. I hate staying in bed."

"You'll be better soon," I told her. "Did you hear that Dana and Jeremy are going to the ninth grade prom together?"

"No. . . ."

"I heard Dana telling Rachel at the bus stop this morning."

"Is she wearing his bracelet again?"

"No, they decided it was the bracelet that was the problem."

"That doesn't make sense. Are you sure you heard right?"

"Yes. I listen to everything they have to say. Besides, she's humming under her breath again."

"The way she did when they first started going out?"

"Yes . . . the same way, only louder."

Alison yawned. "I think I'll take a nap now."

"Okay . . . see you tomorrow."

Jeremy Dragon is back to wearing his chartreuse jacket. He bumped into me in the hallway at school. I saw him coming but he didn't see me and we collided. I suppose I could have stepped aside but I didn't. He knocked my books out of my arms.

"Hey, Macbeth!" he said. "Long time, no see."

"I'm still on your bus."

"Well . . . long time, no notice."

I could smell his breath and his hair and a woodsy scent coming from his shirt as he crouched next to me, helping to gather my books. I got tingles everywhere. Dana is so lucky!

I had trouble concentrating for the rest of the day. I was still thinking about him that afternoon when I got off the bus. Rachel and I were the only ones to get off at Palfrey's Pond. I walked behind her, humming to myself. The crocuses were beginning to bloom. I love the way they work themselves out of the ground. One day there's nothing there and the next, little blue, yellow and white flowers.

Rachel walked with her books under one arm. Her hair bounced up and down, instead of side to side, like Alison's. I thought about catching up with her and saying, *What's new?* But I didn't know how she'd react.

I followed Rachel all the way to her house without thinking. When we got there she turned around and faced me. For a minute I thought she was going to tell me to get lost and I started thinking of what I'd say if she did. But instead her face softened. "I'll walk you home . . ." she said, as if she were asking my permission.

I nodded.

This time we walked next to each other but we didn't speak. When we got to my house I said, "I'll walk *you* home."

Then she nodded. Halfway there I said, "You want to talk about it?"

"Do you?" she asked.

"I don't even remember how it started."

"You told Amber that Max liked me."

"Oh, right . . . I never did get what was so bad about that."

"It was just the last straw," Rachel said. "I was *so* mad at you by then."

"For what?"

"Because you didn't like me anymore."

"No," I said, "you were the one who didn't like me!"

"I didn't like *you* because you didn't like *me!*"

Rachel said. "You were best friends with Alison and everyone knew it."

"But you had Stacey Green," I told her. "You didn't want to be my best friend anymore."

"That's because *you* didn't want to be *mine*!" Rachel shifted her books from one arm to the other. "I felt it was some kind of competition . . . me against Alison . . . and I was always losing."

"You acted like you were too grown-up to hang around with us."

"I was trying to get back at you for leaving me out."

"We never left you out. It was always the three of us."

"I *felt* left out. I *felt* you weren't my best friend anymore."

"You can have more than one best friend at a time," I said.

"No, you can't."

"Why not?"

"Because best means *best*."

I thought about that. "What about close?" I asked. "You can have more than one *close* friend at a time, can't you?"

Rachel thought that over. "I guess so."

"And close is as good as best!"

"I don't necessarily agree," Rachel said.

"But it's better to be friends than not to be friends . . . you agree with that . . . right?"

"Well, yes," Rachel said, "if you're talking about true friends."

"Yes, I'm talking about true friends."

"Then it's definitely better to be than not to be." Rachel stuck her tongue into her cheek. "I think that's a line from Shakespeare," she said.

"I wouldn't know," I told her.

"I hear you got your period," Rachel said.

"Yeah, I did. But only one time, so far."

"And you've lost weight, too."

"I'm not as hungry as I used to be. Mom says my hormones are adjusting."

"Do you still have that stupid poster over your bed?"

"You mean Benjamin Moore?"

Rachel laughed. "I always liked that poster."

"Are you still throwing around big words?"

"You mean literally or figuratively?"

"Ha ha," I said. I had no idea what those words meant.

When we got to Rachel's house we stopped. "I hear you broke up with Max."

"He was a complete airhead," Rachel said. "I hear you're going with Peter Klaff."

"We're not exactly going together. We're friends, is more like it."

Rachel put her books down on the front steps and fished her key out of her bag.

"My father's coming back to work in New York," I said.

"I know. My mother ran into your Aunt Denise."

"Is that how you found out about my parents in the first place?"

"Yes." Rachel unlocked her front door but didn't go inside. "Look . . . I shouldn't have said those things about your parents. I'm sorry. I guess I was trying to hurt you the way you hurt me."

"I never tried to hurt you."

"But you did."

"Then I'm sorry, too," I told her.

"So . . . you want to come to my concert on the fifteenth? I've got a solo."

"Sure."

"You don't *have* to come," Rachel said. "I just want you to know you're invited. And you can bring Alison."

"I don't *have* to bring her."

"No, I want you to. I like Alison."

"Okay, I'll ask her. She's got the flu. I'm on my way to her house now."

"Tell her I hope she feels better."

"I will."

"See you tomorrow," Rachel said.

"Yeah . . . see you tomorrow."

I saw a bee buzzing around the forsythia bush in front of Alison's house. I'll have to start wearing my bee-sting necklace, I thought. I wonder what Alison will say when I tell her Rachel and I are speaking again, that maybe we are even friends. Probably she'll be glad. I broke off a sprig of forsythia and rang Alison's bell.